Edward Tompkins McLaughlin

Literary criticism for students, selected from English essays and ed.

With an introduction and notes

Edward Tompkins McLaughlin

Literary criticism for students, selected from English essays and ed.
With an introduction and notes

ISBN/EAN: 9783337280215

Printed in Europe, USA, Canada, Australia, Japan

Cover: Foto ©Andreas Hilbeck / pixelio.de

More available books at **www.hansebooks.com**

LITERARY CRITICISM
FOR STUDENTS

SELECTED

FROM ENGLISH ESSAYS

AND EDITED

WITH AN INTRODUCTION AND NOTES

BY

EDWARD T. McLAUGHLIN

ASSISTANT PROFESSOR OF ENGLISH
IN YALE COLLEGE

NEW YORK
HENRY HOLT AND COMPANY
1893

CONTENTS.

INTRODUCTION.

It is a delicate problem to adjust the relation between independence and a deference to authority. In *belles lettres*, especially, what seems best to the taste and appreciation of those who are called literary, often fails to please ordinary readers. Subtler phases of thought, heightened style, moods lifted above plain emotions, or plain emotions made great by Wordsworthian simplicity, do not appeal to the majority even of intelligent people. The classics of our poetry and prose are not popular, and where they are read, what to a few appears their best is quite missed by most. These think carelessly, feel bluntly, and are not sensitive to art and beauty. Yet most of them can think and feel, and are in some measure susceptible to æsthetic pleasure. Their difficulty lies in not applying their faculties successfully to literature, or still more, in not taking the trouble to attempt it. Accordingly, they judge inadequately and incorrectly. Well, how far should those who believe that such judgments are partial or mistaken try to impress their own views on the majority—to convert them to their own tastes? Especially in the case of students, is "good taste" to be taught?

There is a certain class of refined people who say that it neither can nor need be. They themselves are acquainted with literature because they like it. If others care for it, let them read it. If not, there is no more reason why they should concern them-selves with books than with bacteriology or harmony or lithology, topics which everyone considers it perfectly proper to leave to specialists. Assumed opinions seem to them like eye-glasses and ear-trumpets for the incurably blind and deaf. What social adventures are so annoying as to fall in with the critical ineptitudes of pinchbeck culture? *Poeta nascitur, non fit;* neither can his audience be manu-factured.

It is to be hoped that this is not the case; at any rate the *laissez faire* of cultivated exclusiveness is not to be commended. People interested in botany or numismatics, for instance, may well enough be indifferent about popular enthusiasm for such sub-jects, but there are the clearest reasons why it is unfortunate, more than unfortunate, for intelligent people not to care about *belles lettres.* Too much profit is lost if they are missed: too much profit, too much pleasure.

One of the pathetic aspects of life is that so large a number never come to realize its inner meaning, or their hidden selves. They would stare in per-plexity at Browning's entreaty to be "unashamed of soul." They move about in a world not realized, spiritual somnambulists. That self-consciousness by which all operations of brain and heart are vital-

ized into a new and finer meaning, is shut away from
them through their want of sensibility. This is true
even of men with brawny intellects that produce
results of great practical value, and also of people
with a kind of heart which is full of amiable utility.
There is a broad difference between what the personal life means even to these, and the enjoyment,
the intelligence, the intensity of it all for such as
contemplate what they see, and dream out of routine
experiences, within and around them, mystery and
beauty. De Musset's career as an individual was
not a satisfactory one, yet it is impossible to think
of it as wholly unenviable when we hear his exclamation, "C'est moi qui ai vécu"—I have lived, I
myself. Now, the incomparable excellence of literature, especially in poetry, is that it penetrates
beneath the crust of life. Commonplaces are translated, and we find ourselves interested by what we
have scarcely noticed. Ideas and sensations are
presented through another medium than the matter-
of-fact. The appeal is made, less to mental than to
sympathetic responsiveness. Beauty of various
kinds is forced upon the attention, until sensibility
becomes more sensitive, and its capacity expands.
Not that literature creates any habitual exaltation,
or that curiously wrought moods hover over our
books. There is nothing especially tangible about
this developed way of looking at things, nor is it in
the least true that such a result is dependent upon
reading. Yet there are multitudes whose finer sense
has been quickened, who have taken a more serious

view of important subjects which mean little when
regarded only trivially, through the aid of the great
writers; to say nothing of their having come to see
their everyday world in pensive twilight sentiment,
as well as in its meridian literalness. There is an
immense difference between the hard pragmatic and
the sympathetic contact with ideas. But how large
a part of literature gives us more than ideas,—sensations. Through it we learn to feel, to feel through
the whole scale of emotion, from soul to verbal form.
Whatever stimulates a refined joy,—stirs the imagination and keeps it abreast with clear sound
sense,—vibrates to the voice of human personality,
instead of being formal, mechanical, and barren
of fruit for fresh warm life, is a part of literature's contribution to human progress. Even the
mere contact with beauty? Certainly the æsthetic
thrill is better than most things the world
gives us.

In the light of such influences, any who are not
anxious to develop appreciation for books, where it
seems wanting, are deficient either in seriousness or
in a sense of responsibility. But it is not easy to
find the way in which this cultivation can be accomplished. Anyone whose profession has brought him
into contact with young men by hundreds, knows to
how many the grace and nicer meaning of poetry
are locked and sealed. The first steps toward the
desired results must be prosaic; people must train
themselves, or be trained, to see what is on the
surface, to grow conscious of metrical differences,

for instance; not to remain quite blind to the real meaning beneath a figurative turn; even to come to recognize that there is a figurative turn. But nothing calls for more tact than how and to what extent to carry on this analysis. Observation and discrimination are indispensable, but literary drill runs a danger of concentrating the attention on fact as an end in itself. In most studies it may be so; in literature it is not.

This scientific age was sure to come to the gates of literary criticism with hands full of method and systematization. Finding how difficult it is to induce students to get at the heart of a poem (and, it may be, sharing in the difficulty themselves), many earnest and well-meaning students have settled upon the close and thorough study of literature from the standpoint of information and analysis. They teach and they make editions with an eye to grammatical, rhetorical, and linguistic instruction. They present clear formulated methods for examining style or argument. They present other authors' exegeses as matter for direct acquisition or as models for application to similar criticism. They annotate texts with elaborate explanations. Their treatment may appear satisfactory: for anyone can memorize, and learn how to apply formulas. It is possible in this way to acquire tangible results, and people are accordingly pleased to think that they are learning; they even may become interested in the details of the study. Especially, ambitious students with little turn for originality make great progress. Yet what does literature mean for them? Superficial knowledge, facts—no soul.

The startling contemporary growth of this so-called scientific study is natural both for teachers and students. As the professional class enlarges, the fascination of the very name of literature and the gentility of the pursuit of it, naturally attract many whose best aptitudes are for acquisition and systematization. There is nothing so much to be feared, by those solicitous for the growth of real culture in this great country's assured destiny of abundant education of some sort, as the ascendency in the departments of literary direction of such mechanically trained scholars. Their methods and industry are hopeless substitutes for inspirations of mind and heart. How inferior they are to that simple-minded absorption of the spirit of our best authors granted even to ordinary men who study them with old-fashioned receptivity. We need to pray for a generation not of minor scholars, but of intimate and sympathetic readers. Let them be less fluent in grammatical and rhetorical arts, and more capable of a quick and happy quotation. Let them be as unconscious of critical phrases and form-ulas of analysis as Shakspere himself was, and instead approach as closely as they may to the thoughts and feelings of his plays. The so-called "laboratory work" in literature may be deferred until scientists introduce literary methods into the laboratory.

So, too, about minute annotation of texts.

Where they can be, allusions, dates, quotations, social or personal side touches, and the like, had better be looked up independently, if the reader desires to know them; and frequently—one almost trembles at the temerity of saying it—he is practically as well off without knowing them. If, for example, a line is quoted, why should the lightly touched passing illustration be made to distract his attention from the subject-matter by an excursus on its author and location? Why should he not go to one of our numerous recent dictionaries for an unusual word? Why should he be taught archeological details or verbal parallels here, while he is trying to learn how to read with his inner thought? A large number of teachers and edited books aim at making scholars, when they ought to try to make good readers. In every calling, technical difficulties become very dear to the practiced and expert workman, and the desire for thoroughness that is really the instinct of a scientific and orderly temperament must answer every question about allusions, origins, and verbal or archeological suggestions. Indeed, there is a place for this; the advanced and special student ought to understand them. It is easy enough to obtain a scholastic equipment when the right time comes. The difficulty is not in using the routine power of brain, but in getting in touch with one's creative consciousness of mind and heart. If the literary neophyte's attention is directed too largely toward facts, he may mistake the means for the end, and as a result of his training find the principal object that confronts him as he takes up new works, nothing spiritual and æsthetic, but only the task of obtaining exterior information, hunting down quotations, dates, and allusions, surveying a poem by the rod and line of a technical phraseology, detecting parallels, and baying at the holes of conjectural originals, finally to emerge from his studies learned, but not literary.

For infinite as is the value of its substance, the essence of literature is beauty. No slight part of its profit rests in the refining influence of its pure loveliness, and in the pleasure which its sweetness and art may add to our lives. To study it mechanically is like grasping a butterfly. It is all there in one's hand, all the "weight and size"; but alas for the one who supposes that this slender, quivering body which he holds is the winged color that flew. And this is just where the mistake is made by those proselytes from Philistia who attempt to conduct educational services in the temple of culture.

The aim, then, for most readers should be to acquire the art of sympathy. The first step toward this, if it does not come naturally, is to read some poem that pleases, until one is thoroughly familiar with it and can call up one and another line here and there, without the book. Then at odd times when one is not in too strenuous a state of mind, to try (if I may employ a word rather poetic for prose) to try musing upon what one remembers of the poem; not disappointed, if no very tangible result shall appear. By and by, when a sentiment has started, through which one begins to have some warmer feeling for the passage, it is well to go over the lines thoughtfully, scrutinizing their meaning, and endeavoring to ascertain the values of minor touches. Poetry should be read aloud, or at least the ear should be trained to follow a silent reading with the closest attention. One of the most interesting and at the same time helpful devices for close knowledge of a piece of literature, is to think out certain topics, such as what clews we find to a knowledge of the author himself; what suggestion we can note of this or that taste or opinion; in what lines his heightened style appears at its best; where he is most happy in fancy, or in cadence. Such topics are interesting and instructive for themselves, and while we consider them we are growing more penetratively familiar with the work before us, without introducing any methods that are mechanical and intrinsically unimportant, if not repellent. Anything, in short, that is sympathetic and personally stimulating, contributing something of richness to our knowledge and feeling of art, thought, and life, is a good exercise in literary analysis. The point of view should be shifting, however, and the treatment flexible.

But although, so far as the primary value of literature goes, facts are nowhere of less importance, there comes a time when a wider and philosophical study is valuable and most interesting: such as observing the forces by which a great period or a great individual has been produced, or inquiring

into the ways whereby schools of letters or single
authors fall short through unfavorable antecedent
or contemporaneous influences; or the biographical
knowledge which adds personal interest to an
author's work, and makes it more intelligible; or a
study of his development, as we follow his writings
chronologically. But large numbers of readers are
not born for such pleasures and privileges, and many
who might enjoy them have too little time; while
others who pursue them miss the central good, by
that old danger of mechanical and harshly intellect-
ualized study. The most laborious students are
frequently the most indolent, so far as interpreting
what they read in terms of their own thought, soul,
and sense for beauty.

Emerson says somewhere that, at a performance
of *Hamlet* to which he had looked forward with
great interest, he noticed nothing after the cry:

> What may this mean,
> That thou, dead corse, again in complete steel
> Revisit'st thus the glimpses of the moon,
> Making night hideous, and we fools of nature
> So horridly to shake our disposition
> With thoughts beyond the reaches of our souls?

Fancy the philosopher poet, his fine face bent
down from the stage and the brilliant theater, as he
sits possessed by the power of the lines, the magic
of their nature touch, the solemn infinitude of
human mystery which they suggest. When a passage becomes in this way our master, absorbing us
with its appeal to heart or mind or sense of art, then

we are getting into the reality of poetry, and the key to it all is the cultivation not of brain, but of sensibility.

The fact that this is so impalpable makes it unteachable. Evidently, too, reading literature so perfectly is unusual and fortuitous. The great advantage of having poetry by heart lies just here, that when we are in the mood for this or that thought or sentiment, it comes to us, and is more a part of ourselves than when we untie it from printed words. Yet if we do not often enjoy such an Emersonian ecstasy, in a lower degree we are constantly susceptible to the vital interpretation of literature, as we more steadily apprehend that our highest study is not to acquire views or facts, but sensations. To this end, we must attend shrewdly, observing even minute details, since one never knows whether there is a secret for him here or there. We must listen for the note of personality. We must relax intellectual rigidity and read sympathetically. If a poem affords no sense of beauty, we must understand that we have read it amiss. To me it seems incomparably better that anyone's accidental moods should be haunted by a subtle or noble thought, or by a line that has soul or music in it, than for one to be a master of learning.

Important as it is that the interpretation should come from within, outside guidance is helpful. Many may receive hints from a comment upon a line, or a development of an author's less obvious traits, through which they will see what they have not seen. To such critical comments as Hudson's, for instance, some of us are increasingly grateful, if for nothing more than the service they did our early reading, in making us feel that there was a moral fascination in passages where our careless perusal had seen nothing. Of all American editors, Hudson (though intellectually unreliable and clumsy, and anything but a great man, save for his sometimes erring love and sympathy) has rendered the best service by stimulating to see the beautiful, not so finely on the side of art, but admirably on the ethical side. "Sign-post criticism" is scoffed at by many who do not need it; but compasses are constantly required, in spite of the world's Giottos.

But then, as readers develop, critics whose discrimination and æsthetic faculty overtop such writers as the one just named afford great pleasure and assistance. When we are thoughtfully familiar with an author we enjoy listening to another and stronger student's comments upon him. Often new ideas are suggested, and we occasionally are quickened into an independent thought by the seemingly accidental stir of mind, perhaps even in resisting a view with which we do not accord. Some critical essays also have the nature of creative literature. There is the liveliest intellectual delight in coming in touch with an elegant and sympathetic mind giving utterance to his sense of the charm and significance of an author whom we ourselves have felt. Even if there is nothing new, we enjoy the play of happy phrase and nimble association; we

enjoy the sense of intelligent and refined companionship. But when a new lode is opened before us,
—meanings and graces unguessed before,—aside
from our absolute acquisition, how profitable is the
sudden discontent with our dull, creeping, inatten-
tion! From interesting criticism, too, the desire
for first-hand knowledge may be acquired, and
convenient, if not at times necessary, guidance
in selection.

But the most profitable criticism is that broad
and philosophical general discussion which is illustrated by such authors as Coleridge or Arnold.
Such passages put us on the track of what we need
to recognize, if we are to appreciate the higher
literature on both its sympathetic and intellectual
sides, without the disadvantage of offering to do
our thinking for us in specific application. They
call our attention to points which, after we have
once noticed them, we find constantly recurring in
our reading. Our literary life is made richer by
observing them. They suggest topics which it is
stimulating to think out. By bringing us in contact
with a more theoretical and æsthetic range of ideas,
they widen our intellectual and artistic world.
They lead our commonplace taste to a just view of
what it is right to admire. Nor is it a trifling
service that they set before us various phases of
the history of literature, one of the most fascinating
and profitable of all studies. Yet in reading even
the most admirable criticism, we need to keep constantly in view our personal relation to literature.

All aids are only instrumental to our close and loving companionship with authors who will make our lives more agreeable, more thoughtful, more sympathetic. Especially in poetry, it is the aim of all study to enable every reader to be his own critic, and thereby ultimately to be, we may say, his own poet. For the finest thoughts, most newly and perfectly apprehended by a great writer's intellect and emotion, and best expressed, realize their highest mission only when the reader becomes to them the creative artist, and takes them up as Shakspere took the crude work of his predecessors; so that by a personal interpretation and heightening, a noble plagiarism, the poetry of thought, feeling, and style is sung by himself to himself alone, in that inner language which we so rarely employ, yet which we surely have employed whenever a poem has flashed from book to brain and soul, and become a mood, a picture, or an inspiration. Yet the levels of literary pleasure are more usual than the heights, and a considerable part of our interest in books is more reflective than emotional. But never unsympathetic; never, if what we call literature is really so, will it yield its best unless we approach it in a spirit not of fact but of sensibility. It will render us more of itself, as we bring to it more of ourselves. Its great gift is in expanding and satisfying our finer nature, and as we grow in refinement of brain and delicacy of feeling, we shall appreciate how well the effort pays of learning it, instead of learning about it. There is a line of Matthew Arnold's, regarding life in general, in which for myself I constantly sum up the true art of interpreting literature:

Think clear, feel deep, bear fruit well.

For surely out of an intimacy of mind and heart with those who have drawn most thought, feeling, and beauty out of life, the fruit of a happier and better character can hardly fail to be born.

The selections that follow are designed to serve as an introduction to literary criticism. Care has been taken to illustrate the characteristic expression as well as thought of the authors represented. To avoid the mechanical tendency of arbitrarily applied opinions, as well as for the larger stimulus of philosophical discussion, a choice has been made of passages that mainly develop general principles, even where they may treat directly of specific authors or works. Where time allows, readers or classes will find constant opportunity for following out suggested topics connected with literary history, and it is hoped that these excerpts may lead to a more extended reading of the authors from whom they are taken. For those, however, to whom such an introduction to criticism is principally directed, close and thoughtful acquisition of a few important ideas seems more profitable than hasty wider reading.

If the views that have been presented in the preceding pages are correct, the first and greatest art to be acquired in literary study is "How to read."

A large majority whose tastes and training have not led them to familiarity with books, find nothing more difficult than learning to observe leading points, and to grasp the essential outlines of a poem or essay. I have met with so many genuine cases of this puzzled confusion as to what should be observed and remembered, that I have appended to the text a few pages containing a partial list of topics involved in the different selections, that may serve to focus the attention for some to whom literary studies are as yet vague and perplexing. Among these will be found such brief explanations of the text as seem necessary, and. not within the reach of most readers' resources; together with a few critical suggestions, and various hints of associated ideas that may profitably be followed out.

It has seemed desirable to give rather more extended passages from two or three authors, and for this fuller exposition of their thought I have selected Coleridge and Arnold, as the two whose influence on the literary criticism of the century has been and still is perhaps most significant. I may add that in the formal study of these examples of English prose, attention should constantly be paid to the literary manner, as well as to the ideas; noting traits of style, and the relation of these to the thought and moral qualities of the writer,

For soul is form and doth the body make.

ENGLISH CRITICISM FOR STUDENTS.

SIR PHILIP SIDNEY.

1554-1586.

[From its historical position Sidney's *Defense of Poesy* is an important work in the development of English criticism. It is one of those inquiries into the nature of poetry that have appealed to philosophical curiosity from classical times down to our own, and that are interesting and suggestive, even if not of the most valuable order. Sidney's work is especially noteworthy as a landmark in the evolution of English prose, and as an indication of the classical spirit of the circle to which he belonged. For he writes more as a student than as an alert contemporary of the men of 1580 ; he was scholastically blind to the signs of the times. Fortunately Marlowe and Shakspere did not take the essay as a literary guide. Yet for a professed classicist, Sidney is not narrow, as his love for English ballads indicates, and his pure and ideal spirit is shown in the serious ethical conception of poetry that marks his entire work.]

From the Defense of Poesy.

IT is not rhyming and versing that maketh a poet (no more than a long gown maketh an advocate, who, though he pleaded in armor, should be an advocate and no soldier) ; but it is that feigning notable images of virtues, vices, or what else, with that delightful teaching, which must be the right describing note to know a poet by. Although, indeed, the senate of poets have chosen verse as their fittest raiment; meaning, as in matter they passed all in all, so in manner to go beyond them; not speaking table-talk fashion, or like men in a dream, words as they chanceably fall from the mouth, but piecing each syllable of each word by just proportion, according to the dignity of the subject.

Now, therefore, it shall not be amiss, first, to weight this latter sort of poetry by his *works*, and then by his *parts;* and if in neither of these anatomies he be commendable, I hope we shall receive a more favorable sentence. This purifying of wit, this enriching of memory, enabling of judgment, and enlarging of conceit, which commonly we call learning, under what name soever it come forth, or to what immediate end soever it be directed; the final end is, to lead and draw us to as high a perfection as our degenerate souls, made worse by their clay lodgings, can be capable of. This, according to the inclination of man, bred many formed impressions; for some that thought this felicity principally to be gotten by knowledge, and no knowledge to be so high or heavenly as acquaintance with the stars, gave themselves to astronomy; others, persuading themselves to be demi-gods, if they knew the causes of things, became natural and supernatural philosophers. Some an admirable delight drew to music, and some the certainty of demonstrations

to the mathematics, but all, one and other, having
this scope to know, and by knowledge to lift up
the mind from the dungeon of the body to the
enjoying his own divine essence.   But when, by the
balance of experience, it was found that the astronomer, looking to the stars, might fall in a ditch ; that
the inquiring philosopher might be blind in himself ;
and the mathematician might draw forth a straight
line with a crooked heart ; then lo! did proof, the
over-ruler of opinions, make manifest that all these
are but serving sciences, which, as they have a private end in themselves, so yet are they all directed
to the highest end of the mistress knowledge, by the
Greeks called ἀρχιτεκτονική, which stands, as I
think, in the knowledge of a man's self ; in the ethic
and politic consideration, with the end of well doing,
and not of well knowing only ; even as the saddler's
next end is to make a good saddle, but his further
end to serve a nobler faculty, which is horseman-
ship ; so the horseman's to soldiery ; and the soldier
not only to have the skill, but to perform the practice of a soldier.   So that the ending end of all
earthly learning being virtuous action, those skills
that most serve to bring forth that, have a most just
title to be princes over all the rest ; wherein, if we
can show, the poet is worthy to have it before any
other competitors.

——I conclude, therefore, that he excelleth history, not only in furnishing the mind with knowledge,
but in setting it forward to that which deserveth to
be called and accounted good : which setting forward,

and moving to well-doing, indeed, setteth the laurel
crown upon the poet as victorious; not only of the
historian, but over the philosopher, howsoever in
teaching it may be questionable. For suppose it
be granted, that which I suppose with great reason
may be denied, that the philosopher, in respect
of his methodical proceeding, teach more perfectly
than the poet, yet do I think that no man is so
much φιλοφιλό σοφος, as to compare the philosopher in moving with the poet. And that moving is
of a higher degree than teaching, it may by this
appear, that it is well-nigh both the cause and effect
of teaching; for who will be taught, if he be not
moved with desire to be taught? And what so
much good doth that teaching bring forth (I speak
still of moral doctrine) as that it moveth one to do
that which it doth teach? For, as Aristotle saith, it
is not γνῶσις but πρά ξις[1] must be the fruit: and
how πρά ξις can not be, without being moved to prac-
tise, it is no hard matter to consider. The philosopher showeth you the way, he informeth you of the
particularities, as well of the tediousness of the way
and of the pleasant lodging you shall have when
your journey is ended, as of the many by-turnings
that may divert you from your way; but this is to
no man, but to him that will read him, and read him
with attentive, studious painfulness; which constant
desire whosoever hath in him, hath already passed
half the hardness of the way, and therefore is be-

---

[1] Not knowledge but practice.

holden to the philosopher but for the other half.
Nay, truly, learned men have learnedly thought that
where once reason hath so much overmastered passion as that the mind hath a free desire to do well,
the inward light each mind hath in itself is as good
as a philosopher's book : since in nature we know it
is well to do well, and what is well and what is evil,
although not in the words of art which philosophers
bestow upon us; for out of natural conceit the
philosophers drew it ; but to be moved to do that
which we know, or to be moved with desire to know,
hoc opus, hic labor est.

' Now, therein, of all sciences (I speak still of
human, and according to the human conceit), is our
poet the monarch. For he doth not only show the
way, but giveth so sweet a prospect into the way, as
will entice any man to enter into it ; nay, he doth,
as if your journey should lie through a fair vineyard,
at the very first give you a cluster of grapes, that
full of that taste you may long to pass further. He
beginneth not with obscure definitions, which must
blur the margin with interpretations, and load the
memory with doubtfulness, but he cometh to you
with words set in delightful proportion, either accompanied with, or prepared for, the well-enchant-
ing skill of music; and with a tale, forsooth, he
cometh unto you with a tale which holdeth children
from play, and old men from the chimney-corner;
and, pretending no more, doth intend the winning
of the mind from wickedness to virtue ; even as the
child is often brought to take most wholesome

things by hiding them in such other as have a pleasant taste; which, if one should begin to tell them the nature of the aloes or rhubarb they should receive, would sooner take their physic at their ears than at their mouth. So it is in men (most of which are childish in the best things, till they be cradled in their graves); glad they will be to hear the tales of Hercules, Achilles, Cyrus, Æneas; and hearing them, must needs hear the right description of wisdom, valor, and justice; which, if they had been barely (that is to say, philosophically) set out, they would swear they be brought to school again.

BEN JONSON.

[1573-1637.]

[Milton's word for Jonson's comedies, "learned," applies to his entire literary career. He stands apart from the other famous Elizabethan dramatists as a representative of classical training and method adapted to the modern age. His scholastic taste never quite approved the romantic unconstraint and, as he felt, extreme spontaneity of his contemporaries. The so-called proprieties of form and treatment seemed to him literary essentials, and even in his lyrics, for many readers the most engaging part of his work, we find numerous traces of classical influence. More than any other author of his day, literature to Jonson was an art, and he devoted his active and trained mind closely to the theory as well as practice of it. Even from his plays we see that he was a critic. In the collection of prose observations called "Discoveries," he has left many admirable discussions of various topics, and the extracts which follow show that he deserves to be remembered as one of our shrewdest general critics as well as one of our foremost lyrical and dramatic poets.]

From the Explorata, or Discoveries.

——To judge of poets is only the faculty of poets; and not of all poets, but the best. *Nemo infelicius de poetis judicavit, quam qui de poetis scripsit.* But some will say critics are a kind of tinkers, that make more faults than they mend ordinarily. See their diseases and those of grammarians. It is true, many bodies are the worse for the meddling with; and the multitude of physicians hath destroyed many sound patients with their wrong practice. But the office of a true critic or censor is, not to throw by a letter anywhere, or damn an innocent syllable, but lay the words together, and amend them; judge sincerely of the author and his matter, which is the sign of solid and perfect learning in a man. Such was Horace, an author of much civility, and, if any one among the heathen can be, the best master both of virtue and wisdom; an excellent and true judge upon cause and reason, not because he thought so, but because he knew so out of use and experience.

——Language most shows a man : Speak, that I may see thee. It springs out of the most retired and inmost parts of us, and is the image of the parent of it, the mind. No glass renders a man's form or likeness so true as his speech. Nay, it is likened to a man; and as we consider feature and composition in a man, so words in language; in the greatness, aptness, sound structure, and harmony of it.

——I cannot think Nature is so spent and decayed that she can bring forth nothing worth her former years. She is always the same, like herself; and when she collects her strength is abler still. Men are decayed, and studies: she is not.

——I know nothing can conduce more to letters than to examine the writings of the ancients, and not to rest in their sole authority, or take all upon trust from them, provided the plagues of judging

and pronouncing against them be away; such as are
envy, bitterness, precipitation, impudence, and scur-
rile scoffing. For to all the observations of the
ancients we have our own experience, which if we
will use and apply, we have better means to pronounce. It is true they opened the gates, and made
the way that went before us, but as guides, not commanders: *Non domini nostri, sed duces fuere.* Truth
lies open to all; it is no man's several. *Patet omnibus veritas; nondum est occupata. Multum ex illa,
etiam futuris relictum est.*

——I could never think the study of wisdom confined only to the philosopher, or of piety to the
divine, or of state to the politic; but that he which
can feign a commonwealth (which is the poet), can
gown it with counsels, strengthen it with laws, correct it with judgments, inform it with religion and
morals, is all these. We do not require in him mere
elocution, or an excellent faculty in verse, but the
exact knowledge of all virtues and their contraries,
with ability to render the one loved, the other hated,
by his proper embattling them. The philosophers
did insolently, to challenge only to themselves that
which the greatest generals and gravest counsellors
never durst. For such had rather do than promise
the best things.

——But the wretcheder are the obstinate contem-
ners of all helps and arts; such as presuming on
their own naturals,[1] which, perhaps, are excellent,

---

[1] Natural talents.

dare deride all diligence, and seem to mock at the
terms when they understand not the things; thinking that way to get off wittily with their ignorance.
These are imitated often by such as are their peers
in negligence though they cannot be in nature; and
they utter all they can think with a kind of violence
and indisposition, unexamined, without relation
either to person, place, or any fitness else; and the
more wilful and stubborn they are in it the more
learned they are esteemed of the multitude, through
their excellent vice of judgment, who think those
things the stronger that have no art; as if to break
were better than to open, or to rend asunder
gentler than to loose.

It cannot but come to pass that these men who
commonly seek to do more than enough may sometimes happen on something that is good and great;
but very seldom: and when it comes it doth not
recompense the rest of their ill. For their jests, and
their sentences, which they only and ambitiously
seek for, stick out, and are more eminent, because
all is sordid and vile about them; as lights are more
discerned in a thick darkness than a faint shadow.
Now, because they speak all they can, however un-
fitly, they are thought to have the greater copy;[1]
where the learned use ever election and a mean,
they look back to what they intended at first, and
make all an even and proportioned body. The true
artificer will not run away from Nature as he were

---

[1] Abundance.

afraid of her, or depart from life and the likeness of
truth, but speak to the capacity of his hearers. And
though his language differ from the vulgar somewhat, it shall not fly from all humanity, with the
Tamerlanes and Tamer-chams of the late age, which
had nothing in them but the scenical strutting and
furious vociferation to warrant them to the ignorant
gapers. He knows it is his only art so to carry
it, as none but artificers perceive it. In the mean
time, perhaps, he is called barren, dull, lean, a poor
writer, or by what contumelious word can come in
their cheeks, by these men who, without labor, judgment, knowledge, or almost sense, are received or
preferred before him. He gratulates them and their
fortune. An other age, or juster men, will acknowledge the virtues of his studies, his wisdom in divid-
ing,' his subtlety in arguing, with what strength he
doth inspire his readers, with what sweetness he
strokes them; in inveighing, what sharpness; in
jest, what urbanity he uses; how he doth reign in
men's affections; how invade and break in upon
them, and make their minds like the thing he writes.
Then in his elocution to behold what word is proper,
which hath ornament, which height, what is beautifully translated, where figures are fit, which gentle,
which strong, to show the composition manly; and
how he hath avoided faint, obscure, obscene, sordid,
humble, improper, or effeminate phrase; which is
not only praised of the most, but commended, which
is worse, especially for that it is naught.

' Analyzing.

——'Custom is the most certain mistress of language, as the public stamp makes the current money.
But we must not be too frequent with the mint, every
day coining, nor fetch words from the extreme and
utmost ages; since the chief virtue of a style is perspicuity, and nothing so vicious in it as to need an
interpreter. Words borrowed of antiquity do lend
a kind of majesty to style, and are not without their
delight sometimes; for they have the authority
of years, and out of their intermission do win
themselves a kind of gracelike newness. But the
eldest of the present, and newest of the past language, is the best. For what was the ancient language, which some men so dote upon, but the
ancient custom? Yet when I name custom, I
understand not the vulgar custom; for that were
a precept no less dangerous to language than life, if
we should speak or live after the manners of the
vulgar: but that I call custom of speech, which is
the consent of the learned ; as custom of life, which
is the consent of the good. Virgil was most loving
of antiquity ; yet how rarely doth he insert *aquai* and
pictai! Lucretius is scabrous and rough in these; he
seeks them: as some do Chaucerisms with us, which
were better expunged and banished. Some words
are to be culled out for ornament and color, as we
gather flowers to straw houses or make garlands;
but they are better when they grow to our style as

---

[1] Cp. Horace *de Arte Poetica ad init.* Also, the extract from
Lowell's Introduction to the *Biglo o Papers* (in the appendix).

in a meadow, where, though the mere grass and
greenness delights, yet the variety of flowers doth
heighten and beautify. Marry, we must not play
or riot too much with them, as in paronomasies;
nor use too swelling or ill-sounding words, *quæ per
salebras, altaque saxa cadunt*. It is true, there is no
sound but shall find some lovers, as the bitterest
confections are grateful to some palates. Our composition must be more accurate in the beginning and
end than in the midst, and in the end more than in
the beginning; for through the midst the stream
bears us. And this is attained by custom, more
than care or diligence. We must express readily and
fully, not profusely. There is difference between
a liberal and prodigal hand. As it is a great point
of art, when our matter requires it, to enlarge and
veer out all sail, so to take it in and contract it is
of no less praise, when the argument doth ask it.
Either of them hath their fitness in the place. A
good man always profits by his endeavor, by his
help, yea, when he is absent; nay, when he is dead,
by his example and memory: so good authors in
their style. A strict and succinct style is that where
you can take away nothing without loss, and that
loss to be manifest.

——For a man to write well, there are required
three necessaries—to read the best authors, observe
the best speakers, and much exercise of his own
style. In style, to consider what ought to be written, and after what manner, he must first think and
excogitate his matter, then choose his words, and

examine the weight of either.   Then take care, in
placing and ranking both matter and words, that
the composition be comely; and to do this with
diligence and often.   No matter how slow the style
be at first, so it be labored and accurate ; seek the
best, andbe not glad of the forward conceits, or
first words, that offer themselves to us; but judge
of what we invent, and order what we approve.
Repeat often what we have formerly written ; which
beside that it helps the consequence, and makes the
juncture better, it quickens the heat of imagination,
that often cools in the time of setting down, and
gives it new strength, as if it grew lustier by the
going back.   As we see in the contention of leaping,
they jump farthest that fetch their race largest ; or,
as in throwing a dart or javelin, we force back our
arms to make our loose the stronger.   Yet, if we
have a fair gale of wind, I forbid not the steering
out of our sail, so the favor of the gale deceive us
not.   For all that we invent doth please us in the
conception of birth, else we would never set it down.
But the safest is to return to our judgment,[1] and
handle over again those things the easiness of which
might make them justly suspected.   So did the
best writers in their beginnings ; they imposed upon
themselves care and industry ; they did nothing
rashly : they obtained first to write well, and then
custom made it easy and a habit.   By little and little
their matter showed itself to them more plentifully ;
their words answered, their composition followed ;

---

[1] Cp. Jonson's criticism of Shakspere, *Explorata*, 71.

and all, as in a well-ordered family, presented itself
in the place. So that the sum of all is, ready writing
makes not good writing, but good writing brings on
ready writing. Yet, when we think we have got the
faculty, it is even then good to resist it, as to give a
horse a check sometimes with a bit, which doth not
so much stop his course as stir his mettle. Again,
whither a man's genius is best able to reach, thither
it should more and more contend, lift and dilate
itself; as men of low stature raise themselves on
their toes, and so ofttimes get even, if not eminent.
Besides, as it is fit for grown and able writers to
stand of themselves, and work with their own
strength, to trust and endeavor by their own faculties, so it is fit for the beginner and learner to study
others and the best. For the mind and memory are
more sharply exercised in comprehending another
man's things than our own; and such as accustom
themselves and are familiar with the best authors
shall ever and anon find somewhat of them in themselves, and in the expression of their minds, even
when they feel it not, be able to utter something
like theirs, which hath an authority above their own.
Nay, sometimes it is the reward of a man's study,
the praise of quoting another man fitly; and though
a man be more prone and able for one kind of writing than another, yet he must exercise all. For as
in an instrument, so in style, there must be a harmony and consent of parts.

JOHN DRYDEN.

[1631–1700.]

[Dryden's dramatization of Paradise Lost appeared in 1674, with this introductory essay on heroic poetry and poetic license. For its length it is the most varied and suggestive of his numerous critical writings, if not so excellent as some that followed it. Respect for Dryden as a critic has been steadily growing during the last two centuries ; what he wrote of Chaucer may with a modification be applied to himself—"He is a fountain of good sense." He was so open minded and progressive all through his life that the study of his criticism becomes especially interesting as an illustration of literary development. His mind was vigorous rather than subtle, and his sympathies were with the Restoration school, at whose head he stands; yet he manifests no little catholicity and sensitiveness. He is moreover one of the most agreeable prose authors in our literature, writing "prose such as we would all gladly use if we only knew how " —easy and clear, entirely unostentatious, with the pleasantest touches of familiarity, and yet not lacking in seriousness and a gentleman's dignity. The passage that follows, aside from the great interest of its literary principles, contains many suggestions about Dryden and his literary generation ; for example, the contemporary estimate of Milton, and Dryden's defence of those lines of his own that correspond more with the taste of his middle than of his later period. Dr. Johnson's prepossession in favor of the classical school does not mar the fairness of his judgment in saying that Dryden is the father of English criticism and that he writes the criticism of a poet.]

The Preface to the State of Innocence.

To satisfy the curiosity of those who will give themselves the trouble of reading the ensuing poem, I think myself obliged to render them a reason why I publish an Opera which was never acted. In the first place, I shall not be ashamed to own that my chiefest motive was the ambition which I acknowledged in the epistle. I was desirous to lay at the feet of so beautiful and excellent a princess,[1] a work which, I confess, was unworthy her; but which I hope she will have the goodness to forgive. I was also induced to it in my own defence, many hundred copies of it being dispersed abroad, without my knowledge or consent ; so that every one gathering new faults, it became at length a libel against me ; and I saw, with some disdain, more nonsense than either I or as bad a poet could have crammed into it at a month's warning ; in which time, it was wholly written, and not since revised. After this, I cannot, without injury to the deceased author of Paradise Lost, but acknowledge that this poem has received its entire foundation, part of the design, and many of the ornaments from him. What I have borrowed, will be so easily discerned from my mean productions, that I shall not need to point the reader to the places : and truly, I should be sorry, for my own sake, that any one should take the pains to compare them together, the original being undoubtedly one of the greatest, most noble, and most sublime poems, which either this age or nation has

---

[1] The Duchess of York.

produced. And though I could not refuse the partiality of my friend,[1] who is pleased to commend me in his verses, I hope they will rather be esteemed the effect of his love to me, than of his deliberate and sober judgment. His genius is able to make beautiful what he pleases: yet, as he has been too favorable to me, I doubt not but he will hear of his kindness from many of our contemporaries: for we are fallen into an age of illiterate, censorious, and detracting people; who, thus qualified, set up for critics.

In the first place, I must take leave to tell them, that they wholly mistake the nature of criticism, who think its business is principally to find fault. Criticism, as it was first instituted by Aristotle, was meant a standard of judging well, the chiefest part of which is to observe those excellencies which should delight a reasonable reader. If the design, the conduct, the thoughts, and the expressions of a poem, be generally, such as proceed from a true genius of poetry, the critic ought to pass his judgment in favor of the author. 'Tis malicious and unmanly to snarl at the little lapses of a pen, from which Virgil himself stands not exempted. Horace acknowledges that honest Homer nods sometimes: he is not equally awake in every line. But he leaves it also as a standing measure for our judgments:

——Non, ubi plura nitent in carmine, paucis
Offendi maculis, quas aut incuria fudit
Aut humana parum cavit natura.——

[1] An extravagant compliment of Lee's to Dryden's supposed improvement on Milton.

And Longinus, who was undoubtedly after Aristotle the greatest critic among the Greeks, in his twenty-seventh chapter περὶ ὕψους, has judiciously preferred the sublime genius that sometimes errs, to the middling or indifferent one which makes few faults, but seldom or never rises to any excellence. He compares the first to a man of large possessions, who has not leisure to consider of every slight expense, will not debase himself to the management of every trifle. Particular sums are not laid out or spared to the greatest advantage in his economy, but are sometimes suffered to run to waste, while he is only careful of the main. On the other side, he likens the mediocrity of wit to one of a mean fortune, who manages his store with extreme frugality, or rather parsimony; but who, with fear of running into profuseness, never arrives to the magnificence of living. This kind of genius writes indeed correctly. A wary man he is in grammar, very nice as to solecism or barbarism, judges to a hair of little decencies, knows better than any man what is not to be written, and never hazards himself so far as to fall; but plods on deliberately, and, as a grave man ought, is sure to put his staff before him. In short, he sets his heart upon it, and with wonderful care makes his business sure; that is, in plain English, neither to be blamed nor praised.——I could, saith my author, find out some blemishes in Homer; and am, perhaps, as naturally inclined to be disgusted at a fault as another man. But after all, to speak impartially, his failings are such as are only marks of human frailty; they are little mistakes, or rather negligences, which have escaped his pen in the fer vor of his writing; the sublimity of his spirit carries it with me against his carelessness. And though Apollonius his Argonautes, and Theocritus his Eidullia, are more free from errors, there is not any man of so false a judgment, who would choose rather to have been Apollonius or Theocritus, than Homer.

'Tis worth our consideration, a little to examine how much these hypercritics of English poetry differ from the opinion of the Greek and Latin judges of antiquity; from the Italians and French, who have succeeded them; and, indeed, from the general taste and approbation of all ages. Heroic poetry, which they contemn, has ever been esteemed, and ever will be, the greatest work of human nature; in that rank has Aristotle placed it, and Longinus is so full of the like expressions, that he abundantly confirms the other's testimony. Horace as plainly delivers his opinion, and particularly praises Homer in these verses:

> Trojani belli scriptorem, maxime Lolli,
> Dum tu declamas Romæ, Præneste relegi;
> Qui, quid sit pulchrum, quid turpe, quid utile, quid non,
> Plenius ac melius Chrysippo et Crantore dicit.

And in another place, modestly excluding himself from the number of poets, because he only wrote odes and satires, he tells you a poet is such an one:

> ——Cui mens divinior atque os
> Magna sonaturum.

Quotations are superfluous in an established truth, otherwise I could reckon up amongst the moderns, all the Italian commentators on Aristotle's book of Poetry; amongst the French, the greatest in this age, Boileau and Rapin; the latter of which is alone sufficient, were all other critics lost, to teach anew the rules of writing. Any man who will seriously consider the nature of an epic poem, how it agrees with that of poetry in general, which is to instruct and to delight, what actions it describes, and what persons they are chiefly whom it informs; will find it a work which indeed is full of difficulty in the attempt, but admirable when 'tis well performed. I write not this with the least intention to undervalue the other parts of poetry; for comedy is both excellently instructive and extremely pleasant: satire lashes vice into reformation, and humor represents folly so as to render it ridiculous. Many of our present writers are eminent in both these kinds; and particularly the author of the Plain-Dealer, whom I am proud to call my friend, has obliged all honest and virtuous men, by one of the most bold, most general, and most useful satires which has ever been presented on the English theatre. I do not dispute the preference of tragedy: let every man enjoy his taste. But 'tis unjust that they who have not the least notion of heroic writing should therefore condemn the pleasure which others receive from it, because they cannot comprehend it. Let them please their appetites in eating what they like; but let them not force their dish on all the table. They who would combat general authority with particular opinion, must first establish themselves a reputation of understanding better than other men. Are all the flights of heroic poetry to be concluded bombast, unnatural, and mere madness, because they are not affected with their excellencies? 'Tis just as reasonable as to conclude there is no day, because a blind man cannot distinguish of light and colors. Ought they not rather in modesty to doubt of their own judgments, when they think this or that expression in Homer, Virgil, Tasso, or Milton's Paradise, to be too far strained, than positively to conclude that 'tis all fustian and mere nonsense? 'Tis true, there are limits to be set betwixt the boldness and rashness of a poet; but he must understand those limits who pretends to judge, as well as he who undertakes to write; and he who has no liking to the whole ought in reason to be excluded from censuring of the parts. He must be a lawyer before he mounts the tribunal; and the judicature of one court, too, does not qualify a man to preside in another. He may be an excellent pleader in the Chancery, who is not fit to rule the Common Pleas. But I will presume for once to tell them, that the boldest strokes of poetry, when they are managed artfully, are those which most delight the reader.

Virgil and Horace, the severest writers of the severest age, have made frequent use of the hardest metaphors, and of the strongest hyperboles: and in this case the best authority is the best argument.

For generally to have pleased, through all ages, must bear the force of universal tradition. And if you would appeal from thence to right reason, you will gain no more by it in effect, than, first, to set up your reason against those authors; and secondly, against all those who have admired them. You must prove why that ought not to have pleased, which has pleased the most learned, and the most judicious : and to be thought knowing, you must first put the fool upon all mankind. If you can enter more deeply than they have done into the causes and resorts of that which moves pleasure in a reader, the field is open, you may be heard. But those springs of human nature are not so easily discovered by every superficial judge : it requires philosophy as well as poetry to sound the depth of all the passions ; what they are in themselves, and how they are to be provoked ; and in this science the best poets have excelled. Aristotle raised the fabric of his poetry from observations of those things in which Euripides, Sophocles, and Æschylus pleased ; he considered how they raised the passions, and thence has drawn rules for our imitation. From hence have sprung the tropes and figures, for which they wanted a name, who first practised them and succeeded in them. Thus I grant you that the knowledge of Nature was the original rule, and that all poets ought to study her, as well as Aristotle and Horace her interpreters. But then this also undeniably follows, that those things which delight all ages must have

been an imitation of Nature; which is all I contend.
Therefore is rhetoric made an art; therefore the
names of so many tropes and figures were invented;
because it was observed they had such and such
an effect upon the audience. Therefore catachreses
and hyperboles have found their place amongst
them; not that they are to be avoided, but to be
used judiciously, and placed in poetry, as height-
nings and shadows are in painting, to make the
figure bolder, and cause it to stand off to sight.

> ——Nec retia cervis
> Ulla dolum meditantur,

says Virgil in his Eclogues. And speaking of
Leander in his Georgicks:

> Nocte natat cæca serus freta; quem super ingens
> Porta tonat cœli, et scopulis illisa reclamant
> Æquora:——

In both of these, you see, he fears not to give voice
and thought to things inanimate.

Will you arraign your master Horace for his hardness of expression, when he describes the death of
Cleopatra? and says she did " Asperas tractare ser-
pentes, ut atrum corpore combiberet venenum?"
because the body in that action performs what is
proper to the mouth.

As for hyperboles, I will neither quote Lucan nor
Statius, men of an unbounded imagination, but who
often wanted the poise of judgment. The divine

Virgil·was not liable to that exception; and yet he describes Polyphemus thus:

> "——Grad-iturque per æquor
> Jam medium ; necdum fluctus latera ardua tinxit."

In imitation of this place, our admirable Cowley[1] thus paints Goliah:

> "The valley, now, this monster seem'd to fill ;
> And we, methought, look'd up to him from our hill."

Where the two words, seem'd and methought, have mollified the figure ; and yet if they had not been there, the fright of the Israelites might have excused their belief of the giant's stature.

In the eighth of the Æneids, Virgil paints the swiftness of Camilla thus:[2]

> Illa vel intactæ segetis per summa volaret
> Gramina, nec teneras cursu læsisset aristas :
> Vel mare per medium, fluctu suspensa tumenti,
> Ferret iter, celeris nec tingueret æquore plantas.

You are not obliged, as in history, to a literal belief of what the poet says: but you are pleased with the image, without being cozened by the fiction.

Yet even in history Longinus quotes Herodotus on this occasion of hyperboles. The Lacedemonians, says he, at the·Straits of Thermopylæ, de-

---

[1] In later writings Dryden condemns this darling of his youth for such extravagant expressions.

[2] At the end of the seventh book. The slight mistake is interesting, since it shows that Dryden is quoting from memory—something indicated also in an earlier passage.

fended themselves to the last extremity ; and when their arms failed them, fought it out with their nails and teeth; till at length (the Persians shooting continually upon them) they lay buried under the arrows of their enemies. It is not reasonable (continues the critic) to believe that men could defend themselves with their nails and teeth from an armed multitude ; nor that they lay buried under a pile of darts and arrows : and yet there wants not probability for the figure, because the hyperbole seems not to have been made for the sake of the description, but rather to have been produced from the occasion.

'Tis true, the boldness of the figures are to be hidden sometimes by the address of the poet, that they may work their effect upon the mind, without discovering the art which caused it; and therefore they are principally to be used in passion, when we speak more warmly, and with more precipitation than at other times. For then, " Si vis me flere, dolendum est primum ipsi tibi;" the poet must put on the passion he endeavors to represent. A man in such an occasion is not cool enough, either to reason rightly, or to talk calmly. Aggravations are then in their proper places ; interrogations, exclamations, hyperbata, or a disordered connection of discourse, are graceful there, because they are natural. The sum of all depends on what before I hinted, that this boldness of expression is not to be blamed, if it be managed by the coolness and discretion which is necessary to a poet.

Yet before I leave this subject I cannot but take notice how disingenuous our adversaries appear : all that is dull, insipid, languishing, and without sinews in a poem, they call an imitation of nature; they only offend our most equitable judges, who think beyond them; and lively images and elocution are never to be forgiven.

What fustian, as they call it, have I heard these gentlemen find out in Mr. Cowley's Odes? I acknowledged myself unworthy to defend so excellent an author, neither have I room to do it here: only in general I will say, that nothing can appear more beautiful to me than the strength of those images which they condemn.

Imaging is in itself the very height and life of poetry. 'Tis, as Longinus describes it, a discourse which, by a kind of enthusiasm or extraordinary emotion of the soul, makes it seem to us that we behold those things which the poet paints, so as to be pleased with them, and to admire them.

If poetry be imitation, that part of it must needs be best which describes most lively our actions and passions, our virtues and our vices, our follies and our humors. For neither is comedy without its part of imaging; and they who do it best are certainly the most excellent in their kind. This is too plainly proved to be denied. But how are poetical fictions, how are hippocentaurs and chimæras, or how are angels and immaterial substances to be imaged; which, some of them, are things quite out of nature; others, such whereof we can have no notion? This

is the last refuge of our adversaries, and more than
any of them have yet had the wit to object against
us. The answer is easy to the first part of it. The
fiction of some beings which are not in nature
(second notions, as the logicians call them) has been
founded on the conjunction of two natures which
have a real separate being. So Hippocentaurs were
imaged by joining the natures of a man and horse
together, as Lucretius tells us, who has used this
word of *image* oftener than any of the poets.

> Nam certe ex vivo Centauri non fit imago,
> Nulla fuit quoniam talis natura animantis :
> Verum ubi equi atque hominis casu convenit imago,
> Hærescit facile extemplo, etc.

The same reason may also be alleged for chimæ
ras and the rest. And poets may be allowed the
like liberty, for describing things which really exist
not, if they are founded on popular belief. Of this
nature are fairies, pygmies, and the extraordinary
effects of magic : for 'tis still an imitation, though
of other men's fancies ; and thus are Shakespeare's
Tempest, his Midsummer Night's Dream, and
Ben Jonson's Mask of Witches to be defended.
For immaterial substances, we are authorized by
Scripture in their description ; and herein the text
accommodates itself to vulgar apprehension, in giving angels the likeness of beautiful young men.
Thus, after the pagan divinity, has Homer drawn
his gods with human faces ; and thus we have notions of things above us, by describing them like
other beings more within our knowledge.

I wish I could produce any one example of excellent imaging in all this poem : perhaps I cannot, but that which comes nearest it is in these four lines, which have been sufficiently canvassed by my well-natured censors :

> Seraph and Cherub, careless of their charge,
> And wanton, in full ease now live at large ;
> Unguarded leave the passes of the sky,
> And all dissolv'd in hallelujahs lie.

I have heard (says one of them) of anchovies dissolved in sauce, but never of an angel in hallelujahs. A mighty witticism ! (if you will pardon a new word,) but there is some difference between a laugher and a critic. He might have burlesqued Virgil too, from whom I took the image :

> "Invadunt urbem, somno vinoque ; sepultam."

A city's being buried is just as proper, on occasion, as an angel's being dissolved in ease and songs of triumph. Mr. Cowley lies as open, too, in many places :

> "Where their vast courts the mother waters keep, etc."

For if the mass of waters be the mothers, then their daughters, the little streams, are bound in all good manners to make curtsey to them, and ask them blessing. How easy 'tis to turn into ridicule the best descriptions, when once a man is in the humor of laughing till he wheezes at his own dull jest ! But an image which is strongly and beautifully set before the eyes of the reader will still be poetry

when the merry fit is over, and last when the other
is forgotten.

I promised to say somewhat of poetic license, but
have in part anticipated my discourse already.
Poetic license I take to be the liberty which poets
have assumed to themselves in all ages, of speaking
things in verse which are beyond the severity of
prose. 'Tis that particular character which distinguishes and sets the bounds betwixt Oratio soluta[1]
and poetry. This, as to what regards the thought
or imagination of a poet, consists in fiction; but
then those thoughts must be expressed; and here
arise two other branches of it : for if this license be
included in a single word, it admits of tropes; if in
a sentence or proposition, of figures; both which
are of a much larger extent, and more forcibly to be
used in verse than prose. This is that birthright
which is derived to us from our great forefathers,
even from Homer down to Ben. And they who
would deny it to us have, in plain terms, the fox's
quarrel to the grapes—they cannot reach it.

How far these liberties are to be extended I will
not presume to determine here, since Horace does
not. But it is certain that they are to be varied according to the language and age in which an author
writes. That which would be allowed to a Grecian
poet, Martial tells you, would not be suffered in a
Roman. And 'tis evident that the English does
more nearly follow the strictness of the latter than

---

[1] Prose,

the freedoms of the former. Connection of epithets, or the conjunction of two words in one, are frequent and elegant in the Greek ; which yet Sir Philip Sidney and the translator of Du Bartas, have unluckily attempted in the English ; though this, I confess, is not so proper an instance of poetic license as it is of variety of idiom in languages.

Horace a little explains himself on the subject of Licentia Poetica in these verses :

> " ——Pictoribus atque poetis
> Quidlibet audendi semper fuit æqua potestas :
> Sed non, ut placidis coëant immitia, non ut
> Serpentes avibus geminentur, tigribus agni."

He would have a poem of a piece ; not to begin one thing and end with another; he restrains it so far that thoughts of an unlike nature ought not to be joined together. That were indeed to make a chaos. He taxed not Homer, nor the divine Virgil, for interesting their gods in the wars of Troy and Italy : neither, had he now lived, would he have taxed Milton, as our false critics have presumed to do, for his choice of a supernatural argument ; but he would have blamed any author who was a Christian, had he introduced into his poems heathen deities, as Tasso is condemned by Rapin on the like occasion ; and as Camoëns, the author of the Lusiads, ought to be censured by all his readers, when he brings in Bacchus and Christ into the same adventure of his fable.

From that which has been said, it may be collected that the definition of wit (which has been so often

attempted, and ever unsuccessfully, by many poets)
is only this, that it is a propriety of thoughts and
words ; or in other terms, thoughts and words ele-
gantly adapted to the subject. If our critics will
join issue on this definition, that we may "convenire
in aliquo tertio ; " if they will take it as a granted
principle, 'twill be easy to put an end to the dispute.
No man will disagree from another's judgment concerning this dignity of style in Heroic Poetry; but
all reasonable men will conclude it necessary, that
sublimest subjects ought to be adorned with the
sublimest, and (consequently often) with the most
figurative expressions.   In the mean time I will not
run into their faults of imposing my opinions on
other men, any more than I would my writings on
their tastes : I have only laid down, and that super-
ficially enough, my present thoughts ; and shall be
glad to be taught better by those who pretend to
reform our poetry.

JOSEPH ADDISON.

[1672-1719.]

[In his own day Addison was held in higher esteem as a
critic than later generations have deemed him to deserve.
His formal critical studies show no especial force or insight.
That refined taste and correctness which always marked him,
certainly appears in his judgments of literature, but frequently
his thoughts are too mild to be stimulating, and we turn
from the papers on Milton, as well as from the various ethical
reflections, to his delicate social satire, or those genial char-
acter-sketches which never lose their charm. Yet all his writing is agreeable, if for nothing more than its exquisite expression—clear, quiet, unobtrusive, finished yet always easy ;
every essay shows, too, the thought and spirit as well as the
language of a cultivated gentleman. This discussion of
taste, from the *Spectator* (No. 409), presents a favorable
specimen of his critical studies.]

From the Spectator.

GRATIAN very often recommends *the fine taste* as
the utmost perfection of an accomplished man. As
this word arises very often in conversation, I shall
endeavor to give some account of it, and to lay down
rules how we may know whether we are possessed of
it, and how we may acquire that fine taste of writing
which is so much talked of among the polite world.

Most languages make use of this metaphor to express that faculty of the mind which distinguishes
all the most concealed faults and nicest perfections

in writing. We may be sure this metaphor would
not have been so general in all tongues, had there
not been a very great conformity between that mental
taste which is the subject of this paper, and that
sensitive taste which gives us a relish for every different flavor that affects the palate. Accordingly we
find there are many degrees of refinement in the
intellectual faculty, as in the sense which is marked
out by this common denomination.

I knew a person who possessed the one in so great
a perfection, that, after having tasted ten different
kinds of tea, he would distinguish, without seeing the
color of it, the particular sort which was offered him;
not only so, but any two sorts of them that were
mixed together in an equal proportion ; nay, he has
carried the experiment so far, as, upon tasting the
composition of three different sorts, to name the par-
cels from whence the three several ingredients were
taken. A man of a fine taste in writing will discern,
after the same manner, not only the general beauties
and imperfections of an author, but discover the
several ways of thinking and expressing himself which
diversify him from all other authors, with the several
foreign infusions of thought and language, and the
particular authors from whom they were borrowed.

After having thus far explained what is generally
meant by a fine taste in writing, and shown the propriety of the metaphor which is used on this occasion, I think I may define it to be *that faculty of the
soul which discerns the beauties of an author with
pleasure, and the imperfections with dislike.* If a

man would know whether he is possessed of this faculty, I would have him read over the celebrated
works of antiquity, which have stood the test of so
many different ages and countries, or those works
among the moderns which have the sanction of the
politer part of our contemporaries. If, upon the
perusal of such writings, he does not find himself
delighted in an extraordinary manner, or if, upon
reading the admired passages in such authors, he
finds a coldness and indifference in his thoughts, he
ought to conclude, not (as is too usual among taste-
less readers) that the author wants those perfections
which have been admired in him, but that he himself wants the faculty of discovering them.

He should, in the second place, be very careful to
observe whether he tastes the distinguishing perfections or, if I may be allowed to call them so, the
specific qualities of the author whom he peruses ;
whether he is particularly pleased with Livy for his
manner of telling a story ; with Sallust for his enter-
ing into those internal principles of action which
arise from the characters and manners of the persons
he describes ; or with Tacitus for his displaying
those outward motives of safety and interest which
give birth to the whole series of transactions which
he relates.

He may likewise consider how differently he is
affected by the same thought which presents itself
in a great writer, from what he is when he finds it
delivered by a person of an ordinary genius. For
there is as much difference in apprehending a
thought clothed in Cicero's language and that of a

common author, as in seeing an object by the light of a taper or by the light of the sun.

It is very difficult to lay down rules for the acquirement of such a taste as that I am here speaking of. The faculty must in some degree be born with us, and it very often happens that those who have other qualities in perfection are wholly void of this. One of the most eminent mathematicians of the age has assured me that the greatest pleasure he took in reading Virgil was in examining Æneas's voyage by the map; as I question not many a modern compiler of history would be delighted with little more in that divine author than in the bare matters of fact.

But notwithstanding this faculty must in some measure be born with us, there are several methods for cultivating and improving it, and without which it will be very uncertain, and of very little use to the person that possesses it. The most natural method for this purpose is to be conversant among the writings of the most polite authors. A man who has any relish for fine writing either discovers new beauties or receives stronger impressions from the masterly strokes of a great author every time he peruses him ; besides that he naturally wears himself into the same manner of speaking and thinking.

Conversation with men of a polite genius is another method for improving our natural taste. It is impossible for a man of the greatest parts to consider anything in its whole extent and in all its variety of lights. Every man, besides those general observations which are to be made upon an author, forms

several reflections that are peculiar to his own manner
of thinking; so that conversation will naturally
furnish us with hints which we did not attend to, and
make us enjoy other men's parts and reflections as
well as our own. This is the best reason I can give
for the observation which several have made, that
men of great genius in the same way of writing
seldom rise up singly, but at certain periods of time
appear together and in a body, as they did at Rome
in the reign of Augustus, and in Greece about the
age of Socrates. I cannot think that Corneille,
Racine, Molière, Boileau, la Fontaine, Bruyère, Bossu,
or the Daciers would have written so well as they have
done, had they not been friends and contemporaries.

It is likewise necessary for a man who would form
to himself a finished taste of good writing to be well
versed in the works of the best critics, both ancient
and modern. I must confess that I could wish
there were authors of this kind who, besides the
mechanical rules, which a man of very little taste
may discourse upon, would enter into the very spirit
and soul of fine writing, and show us the several
sources of that pleasure which rises in the mind upon
the perusal of a noble work. Thus, although in
poetry it be absolutely necessary that the unities of
time, place, and action, with other points of the same
nature, should be thoroughly explained and understood, there is still something more essential to the
art, something that elevates and astonishes the fancy
and gives a greatness of mind to the reader, which
few of the critics besides Longinus have considered.

JONATHAN SWIFT.

1667–1745.

[The deep-seated notion that critical acuteness means the power of discovering faults, that has been already touched upon, is vigorously assailed in these satirical scraps from Dean Swift. The close attention by which the best qualities of an author are realized often involves inevitably the loss of some early illusions that were to his advantage. But that the study of literature means weighing our books in constant balances, with inclination thrown into the counterpoise scale, is one of the most unhappy notions about so-called culture. Bacon's " To weigh and consider " must be coupled with Sir Thomas Browne's warning to " Bring candid eyes unto the perusal of men's works, and let not Zoilism or detraction blast well-intended labors." There is no more unsatisfactory result of literary study than to find one's increase in accuracy of perception involving a fastidiousness that is either afraid or unable to admire. The short extract below from the " Battle of the Books," is followed by another of similar tone from the " Tale of a Tub." If the student will inform himself upon the occasion for Swift's contempt of critics, the contest over the " Letters of Phalaris," he will see that the satirist is struck by his own lash more sharply than were Bentley and his supporters. They were only exposing a classical forgery. But the lesson of positive instead of negative aims in literary study is none the less valuable.]

From the Battle of the Books.

MEANWHILE Momus, fearing the worst, and calling to mind an ancient prophecy which bore no very good face to his children the moderns, bent his flight to the region of a malignant deity called Criticism. She dwelt on the top of a snowy mountain in Nova Zembla; there Momus found her extended in her den, upon the spoils of numberless volumes, half devoured. At her right hand sat Ignorance, her father and husband, blind with age ; at her left, Pride, her mother, dressing her up in the scraps of paper herself had torn. There was Opinion, her sister, light of foot, hoodwinked, and headstrong, yet giddy and perpetually turning. About her played her children, Noise and Impudence, Dulness and Vanity, Positiveness, Pedantry, and Ill-manners. The goddess herself had claws like a cat ; her head and ears and voice resembled those of an ass ; her teeth fallen out before, her eyes turned inward, as if she looked only upon herself.

From the Tale of a Tub.

By the word critic, at this day so frequent in all conversations, there have sometimes been distinguished three very different species of mortal men, according as I have read in ancient books and pamphlets. For first, by this term were understood such persons as invented or drew up rules for themselves and the world, by observing which a careful reader might be able to pronounce upon the productions of the learned, form his taste to a true relish of the sublime and the admirable, and divide every beauty of matter or of style from the corruption that apes it : in their common perusal of books, singling out the errors and defects, the nauseous, the fulsome, the dull, and the impertinent, with the caution of a man that walks through Edinburgh streets in a morning, who is indeed as careful as he can to watch diligently and spy out the filth in his way. These men seem, though very erroneously, to have understood the appellation of critic in a literal sense; that one principal part of his office was to praise and acquit; and that a critic who sets up to read only for an occasion of censure and reproof is a creature as barbarous as a judge who should take up a resolution to hang all men that came before him upon trial.

Again, by the word critic have been meant the restorers of ancient learning from the worms and graves and dust of manuscripts.

Now the races of those two have been for some ages utterly extinct; and besides, to discourse any further of them would not be at all to my purpose.

The third and noblest sort is that of the TRUE CRITIC, whose original is the most ancient of all. Every true critic is a hero born, descending in a direct line from a celestial stem by Momus and Hybris, who begat Zoilus, who begat Tygellius, who begat Etcætera the elder; who begat Bentley, who begat Rymer, and Wotton, and Perrault, and Dennis; who begat Etcætera the younger.

And these are the critics from whom the commonwealth of learning has in all ages received such immense benefits, that the gratitude of their admirers placed their origin in Heaven, among those of Hercules, Theseus, Perseus, and other great deservers of mankind. But heroic virtue itself has not been exempt from the obloquy of evil tongues. For it has been objected that those ancient heroes, famous for their combating so many giants and dragons and robbers, were in their own persons a greater nuisance to mankind than any of those monsters they subdued ; and therefore, to render their obligations more complete, when all other vermin were destroyed, should in conscience have concluded with the same justice upon themselves, as Hercules most generously did, and upon that score procured to himself more temples and votaries than the best of his fellows. For these reasons I suppose it is why some have conceived it would be very expedient for the public good of learning that every true critic, as soon as he had finished his task assigned, should immediately deliver himself up to ratsbane or hemp, or leap from some convenient altitude ; and that no man's pretensions to so illustrious a character should by any means be received before that operation were performed.

Now, from this heavenly descent of criticism, and the close analogy it bears to heroic virtue, it is easy to assign the proper employment of a true ancient genuine critic, which is, to travel through this vast world of writings ; to pursue and hunt these monstrous faults bred within them ; to drag out the lurking errors, like Cacus from his den ; to multiply them like Hydra's heads ; and rake them together like Augeas's dung ; or else drive away a sort of dangerous fowl, who have a perverse inclination to plunder

the best branches of the tree of knowledge, like
those stymphalian birds that eat up the fruit.

These reasonings will furnish us with an adequate
definition of a true critic : that he is a discoverer
and collector of writers' faults, which may be further
put beyond dispute by the following demonstration :
that whoever will examine the writings in all kinds,
wherewith this ancient sect has honored the world,
shall immediately find, from the whole thread and
tenor of them, that the ideas of the authors have
been altogether conversant and taken up with the
faults and blemishes and oversights and mistakes
of other writers : and, let the subject treated on be
whatever it will, their imaginations are so entirely
possessed and replete with the defects of other pens,
that the very quintessence of what is bad does of
necessity distil into their own ; by which means the
whole appears to be nothing else but an abstract of
the criticisms themselves have made.

SAMUEL JOHNSON.

1709–1784.

[Dr. Johnson was the great critic of his day, and much of his criticism is still valuable. Macaulay's remark that he was an excellent judge of compositions fashioned on his own principles, but one of the poorest of critics upon other kinds of poetry, is fairer than many of Macaulay's sweeping remarks. Certainly, Johnson did not feel about imaginative poetry as we do. His instincts were better than his prejudices, but even his instincts inclined to the Restoration and Queen Anne type of verse. What is most to be commended in his critical essays is the sound sense that amounted to a kind of genius, and the energy and clearness of his treatment. His most important literary work, both for style and subject-matter, was written in his later life—the Lives of the Poets. The first of the following selections is from the life of Cowley —Johnson's famous account of the poetical school that he (not very felicitously) called the metaphysical. The second is from the life of Pope, where he compares the two leaders of his chosen poetry. Johnson's characteristic style is here illustrated at its best. It has an old-fashioned and individual strength and dignity that deserve to be called Johnsonian, instead of Macaulay's " Johnsonese "; the favorite antithesis here is something more than the usual mannerism].

From the Life of Cowley.

Wit, like all other things subject by their nature to the choice of man, has its changes and fashions, and at different times takes different forms. About the beginning of the seventeenth century appeared a race of writers that may be termed the metaphysical poets; of whom, in a criticism on the works of Cowley, it is not improper to give some account.

The metaphysical poets were men of learning, and to show their learning was their whole endeavor; but, unluckily resolving to show it in rhyme, instead of writing poetry they only wrote verses, and very often such verses as stood the trial of the finger better than of the ear; for the modulation was so imperfect, that they were only found to be verses by counting the syllables.

If the father of criticism had rightly denominated poetry $\tau\acute{\epsilon}\chi\nu\eta$ $\mu\iota\mu\eta\tau\iota\kappa\acute{\eta}$, *an imitative art*, these writers will, without great wrong, lose their right to the name of poets; for they cannot be said to have imitated anything; they neither copied nature nor life; neither painted the forms of matter, nor represented the operations of intellect.

Those, however, who deny them to be poets, allow them to be wits. Dryden confesses of himself and his contemporaries, that they fall below Donne in wit; but maintains that they surpass him in poetry.

If wit be well described by Pope, as being " that which has been often thought, but was never before so well expressed," they certainly never attained, nor ever sought it; for they endeavored to be singular in their thoughts, and were careless of their diction. But Pope's account of wit is undoubtedly erroneous; he depresses it below its natural dignity, and reduces it from strength of thought to happiness of language.

If, by a more noble and more adequate conception, that be considered as wit which is at once natural and new, that which, though not obvious, is, upon its first production, acknowledged to be just ; if it be that which he that never found it, wonders how he missed ; to wit of this kind the metaphysical poets have seldom risen. Their thoughts are often new, but seldom natural ; they are not obvious, but neither are they just ; and the reader, far from wondering that he missed them, wonders more frequently by what perverseness of industry they were ever found.

But wit, abstracted from its effects upon the hearer, may be more rigorously and philosophically considered as a kind of *discordia concors;* a combination of dissimilar images, or discovery of occult resemblances in things apparently unlike. Of wit, thus defined, they have more than enough. The most heterogeneous ideas are yoked by violence together ; nature and art are ransacked for illustrations, comparisons, and allusions ; their learning instructs, and their subtlety surprises ; but the reader commonly thinks his improvement dearly bought, and though he sometimes admires, is seldom pleased.

From this account of their compositions it will be readily inferred that they were not successful in representing or moving the affections. As they were wholly employed on something unexpected

and surprising, they had no regard to that uniformity
of sentiment which enables us to conceive and to
excite the pains and the pleasure of other minds:
they never inquired what, on any occasion, they
should have said or done; but wrote rather as be-
holders than partakers of human nature; as beings
looking upon good and evil, impassive and at leisure;
as epicurean deities, making remarks on the actions
of men, and the vicissitudes of life, without interest
and without emotion. Their courtship was void of
fondness, and their lamentation of sorrow. Their
wish was only to say what they hoped had been
never said before.

Nor was the sublime more within their reach than
the pathetic; for they never attempted that com-
prehension and expanse of thought which at once
fills the whole mind, and of which the first effect is
sudden astonishment, and the second rational admiration. Sublimity is produced by aggregation,
and littleness by dispersion. Great thoughts are
always general, and consist in positions not limited
by exceptions, and in descriptions not descending to
minuteness. It is with great propriety that subtlety,
which in its original import means exility of parti-
cles, is taken in its metaphorical meaning for nicety
of distinction. Those writers who lay on the watch
for novelty, could have little hope of greatness; for
great things cannot have escaped former observation. Their attempts were always analytic; they
broke every image into fragments; and could no
more represent, by their slender conceits and labored

particularities, the prospects of nature, or the scenes of life, than he who dissects a sunbeam with a prism can exhibit the wide effulgence of a summer noon.

What they wanted, however, of the sublime they endeavored to supply by hyperbole; their amplifications had no limits; they left not only reason but fancy behind them; and produced combinations of confused magnificence, that not only could not be credited, but could not be imagined.

Yet great labor, directed by great abilities, is never wholly lost; if they frequently threw away their wit upon false conceits, they likewise sometimes struck out unexpected truth; if their conceits were far fetched, they were often worth the carriage. To write on their plan, it was at least necessary to read and think. No man could be born a metaphysical poet, nor assume the dignity of a writer, by descriptions copied from descriptions, by imitations borrowed from imitations, by traditional imagery and hereditary similes, by readiness of rhyme and volubility of syllables.

In perusing the works of this race of authors, the mind is exercised either by recollection or inquiry; something already learned is to be retrieved, or something new is to be examined. If their greatness seldom elevates, their acuteness often surprises; if the imagination is not always gratified, at least the powers of reflection and comparison are employed; and in the mass of materials which ingenious absurdity has thrown together, genuine wit and useful knowledge may be sometimes found buried perhaps

in grossness of expression, but useful to those who
know their value; and such as, when they are ex-
panded to perspicuity and polished to elegance, may
give lustre to works which have more propriety
though less copiousness of sentiment.

This kind of writing, which was, I believe, borrowed from Marino and his followers, had been recommended by the example of Donne, a man of very
extensive and various knowledge, and by Jonson,
whose manner resembled that of Donne more in the
ruggedness of his lines than in the cast of his sentiments.

When their reputation was high, they had undoubtedly more imitators than time has left behind.
Their immediate successors, of whom any remem-
brance can be said to remain, were Suckling, Waller,
Denham, Cowley, Clieveland, and Milton.   Denham
and Waller sought another way to fame, by improving the harmony of our numbers.   Milton tried the
metaphysic style only in his lines upon Hobson the
carrier.   Cowley adopted it, and excelled his predecessors, having as much sentiment and more music.
Suckling   neither   improved   versification   nor
abounded in conceits.   The fashionable style re-
mained chiefly with Cowley; Suckling could not
reach it, and Milton disdained it.

From the Life of Pope.

INTEGRITY of understanding and nicety of discern-
ment were not allotted in a less proportion to Dryden
than to Pope.   The rectitude of Dryden's mind was

sufficiently shown by the dismission of his poetical prejudices, and the rejection of unnatural thoughts and rugged numbers. But Dryden never desired to apply all the judgment that he had. He wrote, and professed to write, merely for the people, and when he pleased others, he contented himself. He spent no time in struggles to rouse latent powers; he never attempted to make that better which was already good, nor often to mend what he must have known to be faulty. He wrote, as he tells us, with very little consideration; when occasion or necessity called upon him, he poured out what the present moment happened to supply, and, when once it had passed the press, ejected it from his mind; for when he had no pecuniary interest, he had no further solicitude.

Pope was not content to satisfy; he desired to excel, and therefore always endeavored to do his best; he did not court the candor, but dared the judgment, of his reader, and expecting no indulgence from others, he showed none to himself. He examined lines and words with minute and punctilious observation, and retouched every part with indefatigable diligence, till he had left nothing to be forgiven.

For this reason he kept his pieces very long in his hands, while he considered and reconsidered them. The only poems which can be supposed to have been written with such regard to the times as might hasten their publication were the two satires of " Thirty-eight "; of which Dodsley told me that they were brought to him by the author, that they might be fairly copied. "Almost every line," he said, "was then written twice over; I gave him a clean transcript, which he sent some time afterwards to me for the press, with almost every line written twice over a second time."

His declaration that his care for his works ceased at their publication, was not strictly true. His parental attention never abandoned them; what he found amiss in the first edition, he silently corrected in those that followed. He appears to have revised the "Iliad" and freed it from some of its imperfections; and the "Essay on Criticism" received many improvements after its first appearance. It will seldom be found that he altered without adding clearness, elegance, or vigor. Pope had perhaps the judgment of Dryden; but Dryden certainly wanted the diligence of Pope.

In acquired knowledge, the superiority must be allowed to Dryden, whose education was more scholastic, and who before he became an author had been allowed more time for study, with better means of information. His mind has a larger range, and he collects his images and illustrations from a more extensive circumference of science. Dryden knew more of man in his general nature, and Pope in his local manners. The notions of Dryden were formed by comprehensive speculation; and those of Pope by minute attention. There is more dignity in the knowledge of Dryden, and more certainty in that of Pope.

Poetry was not the sole praise of either, for both excelled likewise in prose ; but Pope did not borrow his prose from his predecessor. The style of Dryden is capricious and varied ; that of Pope is cautious and uniform. Dryden observes the motions of his own mind ; Pope constrains his mind to his own rules of composition. Dryden is sometimes vehement and rapid ; Pope is always smooth, uniform, and gentle. Dryden's page is a natural field, rising into inequalities, and diversified by the varied exuberance of abundant vegetation ; Pope's is a velvet lawn, shaven by the scythe and levelled by the roller.

Of genius, that power which constitutes a poet ; that quality without which judgment is cold and knowledge is inert ; that energy which collects, combines, amplifies, and animates ; the superiority must with some hesitation be allowed to Dryden. It is not to be inferred that of this poetical vigor Pope had only a little, because Dryden had more : for every other writer since Milton must give place to Pope ; and even of Dryden it must be said, that if he has brighter paragraphs, he has not better poems. Dryden's performances were always hasty, either excited by some external occasion or extorted by domestic necessity ; he composed without consideration, and published without correction. What his mind could supply at call or gather in one excursion was all that he sought and all that he gave. The dilatory caution of Pope enabled him to condense his sentiments, to multiply his images, and to accumulate all that study might produce, or chance

might supply.   If the flights of Dryden therefore
are higher, Pope continues longer on the wing.   If
of Dryden's fire the blaze is brighter, of Pope's the
heat is more regular and constant.   Dryden often
surpasses expectation, and Pope never falls below it.
Dryden is read with frequent astonishment, and Pope
with perpetual delight.

This parallel will, I hope, when it is well considered,
be found just; and if the reader should suspect me,
as I suspect myself, of some partial fondness for the
memory of Dryden, let him not too hastily condemn
me; for meditation and inquiry may perhaps show
him the reasonableness of my determination.

WILLIAM WORDSWORTH.

1770–1850.

[The famous preface to the second edition of the Lyrical
Ballads, to which the following extract belongs, was written
while Wordsworth was at the height of his poetic enthusiasm and genius, and before he had secured any appreci-
able recognition for his new poetical departure. English
criticism presents few passages more suggestive than this,
viewed as the great poet's exposition of the literary theory
that for a long time excited so much controversy, or as an
illumination of his own character and work as a poet, or,
again, as a defence of the dignity of poetry, which with
noble simplicity and sincerity the author's entire life main-
tained. This selection is full of topics that deserve to be
closely pondered and illustrated. It is well to be on one's
guard, however, against accepting some expressions without
careful interpretation. In respect to one of his most emphatic assertions, in particular, it may be that Wordsworth's
own best practice does not bear him out. We may possibly
conclude that his view is closely allied with one of his deficiencies as a poet. But it would be hard to point to an
equal number of pages the mastery of which would ensure
so sound and helpful a conception of poetry and of a normal poetic style. The passage is interesting, moreover, as
another illustration of the admirable prose diction of writers
who have been masters in verse, as well as being a reminder
of how much of our best criticism of poetry has come from
poets.]

From the Preface to the Lyrical Ballads.

THE principal object proposed in these poems
was to choose incidents and situations from common

life, and to relate or describe them, throughout, as
far as was possible in a selection of language really
used by men, and, at the same time, to throw over
them a certain coloring of imagination, whereby ordinary things should be presented to the mind in an
unusual aspect ; and, further, and above all, to make
these incidents and situations interesting by tracing
in them, truly though not ostentatiously, primary
laws of our nature: chiefly, as far as regards the
manner in which we associate ideas in a state of
excitement.   Humble and rustic life was generally
chosen, because, in that condition, the essential passions of the heart find a better soil in which they
can attain their maturity, are less under restraint,
and speak a plainer and more emphatic language ;
because in that condition of life our elementary
feelings coexist in a state of greater simplicity,
and, consequently, may be more accurately contemplated, and more forcibly communicated ; because
the manners of rural life germinate from those elementary feelings, and, from the necessary character
of rural occupations, are more easily comprehended,
and are more durable ; and, lastly, because in that
condition the passions of men are incorporated with
the beautiful and permanent forms of Nature.   The
language, too, of these men has been adopted (purified indeed from what appear to be its real defects,
from all lasting and rational causes of dislike or disgust) because such men hourly communicate with
the best objects from which the best part of language is originally derived ; and because, from their

rank in society and the sameness and narrow circle of their intercourse, being less under the influence of social vanity, they convey their feelings and notions in simple and unelaborated expressions. Accordingly, such a language, arising out of repeated experience and regular feelings, is a more permanent, and a far more philosophical language, than that which is frequently substituted for it by poets, who think that they are conferring honor upon themselves and their art, in proportion as they separate themselves from the sympathies of men, and indulge in arbitrary and capricious habits of expression, in order to furnish food for fickle tastes, and fickle appetites, of their own creation.[1]

I cannot, however, be insensible to the present outcry against the triviality and meanness, both of thought and language, which some of my contemporaries have occasionally introduced into their metrical compositions ; and I acknowledge that this defect, where it exists, is more dishonorable to the writer's own character than false refinement or arbitrary innovation, though I should contend at the same time, that it is far less pernicious in the sum of its consequences. From such verses the poems in these volumes will be found distinguished at least by one mark of difference, that each of them has a worthy *purpose.* Not that I always began to write with a distinct purpose formally conceived ; but

---

[1] It is worth while here to observe, that the affecting parts of Chaucer are almost always expressed in language pure and universally intelligible even to this day.

habits of meditation have, I trust, so prompted and
regulated my feelings, that my descriptions of such
objects as strongly excite those feelings, will be
found to carry along with them a *purpose.* If this
opinion be erroneous, I can have little right to the
name of a poet. For all good poetry is the spontaneous overflow of powerful feelings : and though
this be true, poems to which any value can be
attached were never produced on any variety of
subjects but by a man who, being possessed of more
than unusual organic sensibility, had also thought
long and deeply. For our continued influxes of
feeling are modified and directed by our thoughts,
which are indeed the representatives of all our past
feelings ; and, as by contemplating the relation of
these general representatives to each other, we discover what is really important to men, so, by the
repetition and continuance of this act, our feelings
will be connected with important subjects, till at
length, if we be originally possessed of much sensibility, such habits of mind will be produced, that, by
obeying blindly and mechanically the impulses of
these habits, we shall describe objects, and utter
sentiments, of such a nature, and in such connection with each other, that the understanding of the
reader must necessarily be in some degree enlight-
ened, and his affections strengthened and purified.

It has been said that each of these poems has a
purpose. Another circumstance must be mentioned
which distinguishes these poems from the popular
poetry of the day: it is this, that the feeling therein

developed gives importance to the action and situation, and not the action and situation to the feeling.

A sense of false modesty shall not prevent me from asserting that the reader's attention is pointed to this mark of distinction, far less for the sake of these particular poems than from the general importance of the subject. The subject is indeed important! For the human mind is capable of being excited without the application of gross and violent stimulants; and he must have a very faint perception of its beauty and dignity who does not know this, and who does not further know, that one being is elevated above another, in proportion as he possesses this capability. It has therefore appeared to me, that to endeavor to produce or enlarge this capability is one of the best services in which, at any period, a writer can be engaged; but this service, excellent at all times, is especially so at the present day. For a multitude of causes, unknown to former times, are now acting with a combined force to blunt the discriminating powers of the mind, and, unfitting it for all voluntary exertion, to reduce it to a state of almost savage torpor. The most effective of these causes are the great national events which are daily taking place, and the increasing accumulation of men in cities, where the uniformity of their occupations produces a craving for extraordinary incident, which the rapid communication of intelligence hourly gratifies. To this tendency of life and manners the literature and theatrical exhibitions of the country have conformed themselves. The in-

valuable works of our elder writers, I had almost
said the works of Shakspeare and Milton, are driven
into neglect by frantic novels, sickly and stupid German Tragedies, and deluges of idle and extravagant
stories in verse.—When I think upon this degrading
thirst after outrageous stimulation, I am almost
ashamed to have spoken of the feeble endeavor
made in these volumes to counteract it; and, reflect-
ing upon the magnitude of the general evil, I should
be oppressed with no dishonorable melancholy, had
I not a deep impression of certain inherent and indestructible qualities of the human mind, and likewise of certain powers in the great and permanent
objects that act upon it, which are equally inherent
and indestructible; and were there not added to
this impression a belief, that the time is approach-
ing when the evil will be systematically opposed, by
men of greater powers, and with far more distinguished success.

Having dwelt thus long on the subjects and aim
of these poems, I shall request the reader's permission to apprise him of a few circumstances re-
lating to their *style*, in order, among other reasons,
that he may not censure me for not having performed what I never attempted. The reader will
find that personifications of abstract ideas rarely
occur in these volumes; and are utterly rejected, as
an ordinary device to elevate the style, and raise it
above prose. My purpose was to imitate, and, as
far as possible, to adopt the very language of men;
and assuredly such personifications do not make

any natural or regular part of that language. They
are, indeed, a figure of speech occasionally prompted
by passion, and I have made use of them as such;
but have endeavoured utterly to reject them as a
mechanical device of style, or as a family language
which writers in metre seem to lay claim to by pre-
scription. I have wished to keep the reader in the
company of flesh and blood, persuaded that by so
doing I shall interest him. Others who pursue a
different track will interest him likewise; I do not
interfere with their claim, but wish to prefer a claim
of my own. There will also be found in these
volumes little of what is usually called poetic diction; as much pains has been taken to avoid it as is
ordinarily taken to produce it; this has been done
for the reason already alleged, to bring my language
near to the language of men; and further, because
the pleasure which I have proposed to myself to
impart is of a kind very different from that which
is supposed by many persons to be the proper object of poetry. Without being culpably particular,
I do not know how to give my reader a more exact
notion of the style in which it was my wish and intention to write, than by informing him that I have
at all times endeavoured to look steadily at my subject; consequently, there is I hope in these poems
little falsehood of description, and my ideas are expressed in language fitted to their respective importance. Something must have been gained by
this practice, as it is friendly to one property of all
good poetry, namely, good sense: but it has neces-

sarily cut me off from a large portion of phrases and
figures of speech which from father to son have long
been regarded as the common inheritance of Poets.
I have also thought it expedient to restrict myself
still further, having abstained from the use of many
expressions, in themselves proper and beautiful, but
which have been foolishly treated by bad poets, till
such feelings of disgust are connected with them as
it is scarcely possible by any art of association to
overpower.

If in a Poem there should be found a series of
lines, or even a single line, in which the language,
though naturally arranged, and according to the
strict laws of metre, does not differ from that of
prose, there is a numerous class of critics, who, when
they stumble upon these prosaisms, as they call
them, imagine that they have made a notable discovery, and exult over the poet as over a man ignorant of his own profession. Now these men would
establish a canon of criticism which the reader will
conclude he must utterly reject, if he wishes to be
pleased with these volumes. And it would be a
most easy task to prove to him, that not only the
language of a large portion of every good poem,
even of the most elevated character, must necessarily, except with reference to the metre, in no
respect differ from that of good prose, but likewise
that some of the most interesting parts of the best
poems will be found to be strictly the language of
prose, when prose is well written. The truth of this
assertion might be demonstrated by innumerable

passages from almost all the poetical writings, even
of Milton himself. To illustrate the subject in a
general manner, I will here adduce a short composition of Gray, who was at the head of those who, by
their reasonings, have attempted to widen the space
of separation betwixt prose and metrical composition, and was more than any other man curiously
elaborate in the structure of his own poetic diction.

> In vain to me the smiling mornings shine,
> And reddening Phœbus lifts his golden fire :
> The birds in vain their amorous descant join,
> Or cheerful fields resume their green attire.
> These ears, alas ! for other notes repine ;
> *A different object do these eyes require ;*
> *My lonely anguish melts no heart but mine ;*
> *And in my breast the imperfect joys expire :*
> Yet morning smiles the busy race to cheer,
> And new-born pleasure brings to happier men ;
> The fields to all their wonted tribute bear ;
> To warm their little loves the birds complain.
> *I fruitless mourn to him that cannot hear,*
> *And weep the more because I weep in vain.*

It will easily be perceived, that the only part of
this sonnet which is of any value is the lines printed
in italics ; it is equally obvious, that, except in the
rhyme, and in the use of the single word ' fruitless '
for fruitlessly, which is so far a defect, the language
of these lines does in no respect differ from that of
prose.

By the foregoing quotation it has been shown that
the language of prose may yet be well adapted to
poetry ; and it was previously asserted, that a large
portion of the language of every good poem can in

no respect differ from that of good prose. We will
go further. It may be safely affirmed, that there
neither is, nor can be, any *essential* difference between the language of prose and metrical composition. We are fond of tracing the resemblance
between poetry and painting, and, accordingly, we
call them sisters: but where shall we find bonds of
connection sufficiently strict to typify the affinity
betwixt metrical and prose composition? They
both speak by and to the same organs; the bodies
in which both of them are clothed may be said to
be of the same substance, their affections are kindred, and almost identical, not necessarily differing
even in degree; poetry[1] sheds no tears "such as
angels weep," but natural and human tears; she
can boast of no celestial ichor that distinguishes her
vital juices from those of prose; the same human
blood circulates through the veins of them both.

If it be affirmed that rhyme and metrical arrangement of themselves constitute a distinction which
overturns what has just been said on the strict affinity
of metrical language with that of prose, and paves
the way for other artificial distinctions which the

---

[1] I here use the word " Poetry " (though against my own judgment) as opposed to the word Prose, and synonymous with metrical composition.   But much confusion has been introduced into
criticism by this contradistinction of Poetry and Prose, instead of
the more philosophical one of Poetry and Matter of Fact, or
Science.   The only strict antithesis to Prose is Metre; nor is this,
in truth, a *strict* antithesis, because lines and passages of metre so
naturally occur in writing prose, that it would be scarcely possible
to avoid them, even were it desirable.

mind voluntarily admits, I answer that the language of such poetry as is here recommended is, as far as is possible, a selection of the language really spoken by men; that this selection, wherever it is made with true taste and feeling, will of itself form a distinction far greater than would at first be imagined, and will entirely separate the composition from the vulgarity and meanness of ordinary life; and, if metre be superadded thereto, I believe that a dissimilitude will be produced altogether sufficient for the gratification of a rational mind. What other distinction would we have? Whence is it to come? And where is it to exist? Not, surely, where the poet speaks through the mouths of his characters: it cannot be necessary here, either for elevation of style, or any of its supposed ornaments: for, if the poet's subject be judiciously chosen, it will naturally, and upon fit occasion, lead him to passions the language of which, if selected truly and judiciously, must necessarily be dignified and variegated, and alive with metaphors and figures. I forbear to speak of an incongruity which would shock the intelligent reader, should the poet interweave any foreign splendor of his own with that which the passion naturally suggests: it is sufficient to say that such addition is unnecessary. And, surely, it is more probable that those passages, which with propriety abound with metaphors and figures, will have their due effect, if, upon other occasions where the passions are of a milder character, the style also be subdued and temperate.

But, as the pleasure which I hope to give by the poems now presented to the reader must depend entirely on just notions upon this subject, and as it is in itself of high importance to our taste and moral feelings, I cannot content myself with these detached remarks. And if, in what I am about to say, it shall appear to some that my labor is unnecessary, and that I am like a man fighting a battle without enemies, such persons may be reminded, that, whatever be the language outwardly holden by men, a practical faith in the opinions which I am wishing to establish is almost unknown. If my conclusions are admitted, and carried as far as they must be carried if admitted at all, our judgments concerning the works of the greatest poets both ancient and modern will be far different from what they are at present, both when we praise and when we censure: and our moral feelings influencing and influenced by these judgments will, I believe, be corrected and purified.

Taking up the subject, then, upon general grounds, let me ask, what is meant by the word poet? What is a poet? To whom does he address himself? And what language is to be expected from him? He is a man speaking to men: a man, it is true, endowed with more lively sensibility, more enthusiasm and tenderness, who has a greater knowledge of human nature, and a more comprehensive soul, than are supposed to be common among mankind; a man pleased with his own passions and volitions, and who rejoices more than other men in the spirit of life that is in him; delighting to con-

template similar volitions and passions as manifested
in the goings-on of the universe, and habitually
impelled to create them where he does not find
them. To these qualities he has added a disposi-
tion to be affected more than other men by absent
things as if they were present ; an ability of conjur-
ing up in himself passions, which are indeed far from
being the same as those produced by real events, yet
(especially in those parts of the general sympathy
which are pleasing and delightful) do more nearly
resemble the passions produced by real events, than
anything which, from the motions of their own
minds merely, other men are accustomed to feel in
themselves ;—whence, and from practice, he has
acquired a greater readiness and power in expressing what he thinks and feels, and especially those
thoughts and feelings which, by his own choice, or
from the structure of his own mind, arise in him
without immediate external excitement.

But whatever portion of this faculty we may suppose even the greatest poet to possess, there cannot
be a doubt that the language which it will suggest
to him must often, in liveliness and truth, fall short
of that which is uttered by men in real life, under
the actual pressure of those passions, certain shadows of which the poet thus produces, or feels to be
produced, in himself.

However exalted a notion we would wish to cher-
ish of the character of a poet, it is obvious that
while he describes and imitates passions, his employment is in some degree mechanical, compared with

the freedom and power of real and substantial action and suffering. So that it will be the wish of the poet to bring his feelings near to those of the persons whose feelings he describes; nay, for short spaces of time, perhaps, to let himself slip into an entire delusion, and even confound and identify his own feelings with theirs; modifying only the language which is thus suggested to him by a consideration that he describes for a particular purpose, that of giving pleasure. Here, then, he will apply the principle of selection which has been already insisted upon. He will depend upon this for removing what would otherwise be painful or disgusting in the passion; he will feel that there is no necessity to trick out or to elevate nature; and the more industriously he applies this principle, the deeper will be his faith that no words, which *his* fancy or imagination can suggest, will be to be compared with those which are the emanations of reality and truth.

But it may be said by those who do not object to the general spirit of these remarks, that, as it is impossible for the poet to produce upon all occasions language as exquisitely fitted for the passion as that which the real passion itself suggests, it is proper that he should consider himself as in the situation of a translator, who does not scruple to substitute excellencies of another kind for those which are unattainable by him; and endeavors occasionally to surpass his original, in order to make some amends for the general inferiority to which he feels that he

must submit. But this would be to encourage idle-
ness and unmanly despair. Further, it is the language of men who speak of what they do not understand ; who talk of poetry as of a matter of amusement and idle pleasure ; who will converse with us
as gravely about a *taste* for poetry, as they express
it, as if it were a thing as indifferent as a taste for
rope-dancing, or Frontiniac or Sherry. Aristotle, I
have been told, has said, that poetry is the most
philosophic of all writing: it is so: its object is
truth, not individual and local, but general, and
operative; not standing upon external testimony,
but carried alive into the heart by passion; truth
which is its own testimony, which gives competence
and confidence to the tribunal to which it appeals,
and receives them from the same tribunal. Poetry
is the image of man and nature. The obstacles
which stand in the way of the fidelity of the
biographer and historian, and of their consequent
utility, are incalculably greater than those which are
to be encountered by the poet who comprehends
the dignity of his art. The poet writes under one
restriction only, namely, the necessity of giving immediate pleasure to a human being possessed of that
information which may be expected from him, not
as a lawyer, a physician, a mariner, an astronomer,
or a natural philosopher, but as a Man. Except
this one restriction, there is no object standing between the poet and the image of things ; between
this, and the biographer and historian, there are a
thousand.

Nor let this necessity of producing immediate
pleasure be considered as a degradation of the poet's
art. It is far otherwise. It is an acknowledgment
of the beauty of the universe, an acknowledgment
the more sincere, because not formal, but indirect ;
it is a task light and easy to him who looks at the
world in the spirit of love : further, it is a homage
paid to the native and naked dignity of man, to the
grand elementary principle of pleasure, by which he
knows, and feels, and lives, and moves. We have
no sympathy but what is propagated by pleasure.
I would not be misunderstood ; but wherever we
sympathize with pain, it will be found that the sympathy is produced and carried on by subtile combinations with pleasure. We have no knowledge, that
is, no general principles drawn from the contemplation of particular facts, but what has been built up
by pleasure, and exists in us by pleasure alone.
The man of science, the chemist and mathematician, whatever difficulties and disgusts they may
have had to struggle with, know and feel this.
However painful may be the objects with which the
anatomist's knowledge is connected, he feels that
his knowledge is pleasure ; and where he has no
pleasure he has no knowledge. What then does the
poet? He considers man and the objects that sur-
round him as acting and reacting upon each other,
so as to produce an infinite complexity of pain and
pleasure ; he considers man in his own nature and
in his ordinary life as contemplating this with a certain quantity of immediate knowledge, with certain

convictions, intuitions, and deductions, which from
habit acquire the quality of intuitions ; he considers
him as looking upon this complex scene of ideas
and sensations, and finding everywhere objects that
immediately excite in him sympathies which, from
the necessities of his nature, are accompanied by an
overbalance of enjoyment.

To this knowledge which all men carry about with
them, and to these sympathies in which, without any
other discipline than that of our daily life, we are
fitted to take delight, the poet principally directs
his attention. He considers man and nature as essentially adapted to each other, and the mind of
man as naturally the mirror of the fairest and most
interesting properties of nature. And thus the
poet, prompted by this feeling of pleasure, which
accompanies him through the whole course of his
studies, converses with general nature, with affections
akin to those which, through labor and length of time,
the man of science has raised up in himself, by con-
versing with those particular parts of nature which
are the objects of his studies. The knowledge both
of the poet and the man of science is pleasure ; but
the knowledge of the one cleaves to us as a necessary
part of our existence, our natural and unalienable
inheritance ; the other is a personal and individual
acquisition, slow to come to us, and by no habitual
and direct sympathy connecting us with our fellow-
beings. The man of science seeks truth as a remote
and unknown benefactor; he cherishes and loves it
in his solitude : the poet, singing a song in which all

human beings join with him, rejoices in the presence
of truth as our visible friend and hourly companion.
Poetry is the breath and finer spirit of all knowledge;
it is the impassioned expression which is in the
countenance of all science. Emphatically may it be
said of the poet, as Shakespeare hath said of man,
"that he looks before and after." He is the rock
of defence for human nature; an upholder and pre-
server, carrying everywhere with him relationship
and love. In spite of difference of soil and climate,
of language and manners, of laws and customs: in
spite of things silently gone out of mind, and things
violently destroyed; the poet binds together by
passion and knowledge the vast empire of human
society, as it is spread over the whole earth, and over
all time. The objects of the poet's thoughts are
everywhere; though the eyes and senses of man
are, it is true, his favorite guides, yet he will follow
wheresoever he can find an atmosphere of sensation
in which to move his wings. Poetry is the first and
last of all knowledge—it is as immortal as the heart
of man. If the labors of men of science should ever
create any material revolution, direct or indirect, in
our condition, and in the impressions which we habitually receive, the poet will sleep then no more
than at present; he will be ready to follow the steps
of the man of science, not only in those general indirect effects, but he will be at his side, carrying
sensation into the midst of the objects of the science
itself. The remotest discoveries of the chemist,
the botanist, or mineralogist will be as proper ob-

jects of the poet's art as any upon which it can be
employed, if the time should ever come when these
things shall be familiar to us, and the relations under
which they are contemplated by the followers of
these respective sciences shall be manifestly and
palpably material to us as enjoying and suffering
beings. If the time should ever come when what is
now called science, thus familiarized to men, shall be
ready to put on, as it were, a form of flesh and blood,
the poet will lend his divine spirit to aid the trans-
figuration, and will welcome the being thus produced, as a dear and genuine inmate of the household of man. It is not, then, to be supposed that
any one, who holds that sublime notion of poetry
which I have attempted to convey, will break in
upon the sanctity and truth of his pictures by transitory and accidental ornaments, and endeavor to excite admiration of himself by arts, the necessity of
which must manifestly depend upon the assumed
meanness of his subjeet.

SAMUEL TAYLOR COLERIDGE.

[1772-1834.]

[The tendency to social grouping of leaders of an epoch-making literary school is illustrated in the close association and friendship between Wordsworth and Coleridge. They were mutually appreciative and stimulating, and some of the most critical months of their poetical lives were passed in almost constant companionship. By virtue of his moral strength and seriousness Wordsworth's accomplished work easily outranks his friend's, but Coleridge's natural poetic instincts were broader and more ideal. Accordingly his criticism of the Wordsworthian theory of poetry is of especial value, both for his sympathetic insight into its greatness and beauty, and not less for his recognition of its limitations. The following selections are interesting, aside from their importance as a discussion of the question of poetic diction, from their relation to the famous Lake school chapter of poetical history. Three other extracts from Coleridge's critical writings are also given, which amply justify the rank that has long been assigned him at the head of philosophical literary criticism. Though his metrical style is perhaps the most perfect of any of our modern poets, the diction of his prose is less to be commended. Nor in prose any more than in poetry did Coleridge ever build up to his own plans, and the *Biographia Literaria*, from which these passages come, is not the work that he might have made it. But the literary student finds mingled with its metaphysics many additional literary and æsthetic discussions of great value. His lectures on Shakspere and other dramatists and poets, though fragmentary, are full of thought and a great poet's appreciativeness.

Readers who are interested in comparative studies may find a suggestive topic in the relation of his criticism to that of German writers, especially Schlegel.]

From the Biographia Literaria. Chapter 1.

AT school I enjoyed the inestimable advantage of a very sensible, though at the same time a very severe, master.[1] He early moulded my taste to the preference of Demosthenes to Cicero, of Homer and Theocritus to Virgil, and again Virgil to Ovid. He habituated me to compare Lucretius (in such extracts as I then read), Terence, and, above all, the chaster poems of Catullus, not only with the Roman poets of the so-called silver and brazen ages, but with even those of the Augustan era; and on grounds of plain sense and universal logic, to see and assert the superiority of the former, in the truth and nativeness, both of their thoughts and diction. At the same time that we were studying the Greek tragic poets, he made us read Shakespeare and Milton as lessons: and they were lessons, too, which required most time and trouble to *bring up*, so as to escape his censure. I learnt from him that poetry, even that of the loftiest and, seemingly, that of the wildest odes, had a logic of its own, as severe as that of science; and more difficult, because more subtle, more complex, and dependent on more and more fugitive causes. In the truly great poets, he would say, there is a reason assignable, not only for every word, but for the position of every word;

---

[1] The Rev. James Boyer, many years Head Master of the Grammar School, Christ's Hospital.

and I well remember, that, availing himself of the synonymes to the Homer of Didymus, he made us attempt to show, with regard to each, *why* it would not have answered the same purpose, and *wherein* consisted the peculiar fitness of the word in the original text.

In our own English compositions (at least for the last three years of our school education) he showed no mercy to phrase, metaphor, or image unsupported by a sound sense, or where the same sense might have been conveyed with equal force and dignity in plainer words. Lute, harp, and lyre; muse, muses, and inspirations; Pegasus, Parnassus, and Hippocrene,—were all an abomination to him. In fancy, I can almost hear him now, exclaiming, *"Harp? Harp? Lyre? Pen and ink, boy, you mean! Muse, boy, Muse? Your Nurse's daughter, you mean! Pierian spring? Oh, ay! the cloister-pump, I suppose!"* Nay, certain introductions, similes, and examples were placed by name on a list of interdiction. Among the similes there was, I remember, that of the Manchineel fruit, as suiting equally well with too many subjects; in which, however, it yielded the palm at once to the example of Alexander and Clytus, which was equally good and apt, whatever might be the theme. Was it Ambition? Alexander and Clytus! Flattery? Alexander and Clytus! Anger? Drunkenness? Pride? Friendship? Ingratitude? Late repentance? Still, still Alexander and Clytus! At length, the praises of agriculture having been exemplified in the sagacious observation that, had Alexander been holding the plough, he would not have run his friend Clytus through with a spear, this tried and serviceable old friend was banished by public edict *in secula seculorum.* I have sometimes ventured to think that a list of this kind, or an index expurgatorius of certain well-known and ever-returning phrases, both introductory and transitional, including the large assortment of modest egotisms, and flattering illeisms, etc., etc., might be hung up in our law-courts, and both houses of parliament, with great advantage to the public, as an important saving of national time, an incalculable relief to his Majesty's ministers, but, above all, as ensuring the thanks of the country attorneys and their clients, who have private bills to carry through the house.

Be this as it may, there was one custom of our master which I cannot pass over in silence, because I think it imitable and worthy of imitation. He would often permit our theme exercises, under some pretext of want of time, to accumulate, till each lad had four or five to be looked over. Then placing the whole number *abreast* on his desk, he would ask the writer why this or that sentence might not have found as appropriate a place under this or that thesis: and if no satisfying answer could be returned, and two faults of the same kind were found in one exercise, the irrevocable verdict followed; the exercise was torn up, and another on the same subject to be produced in addition to the tasks of the day. The reader will, I trust, excuse this

tribute of recollection to a man whose severities,
even now, not seldom furnish the dreams by which
the blind fancy would fain interpret to the mind the
painful sensations of distempered sleep, but neither
lessen nor dim the deep sense of my moral and
intellectual obligations.   He sent us to the University excellent Latin and Greek scholars, and tolerable
Hebraists.   Yet our classical knowledge was the
least of the good gifts which we derived from his
zealous and conscientious tutorage.   He is now
gone to his final reward, full of years, and full of
honors, even of those honors which were dearest to
his heart, as gratefully bestowed by that school, and
still binding him to the interests of that school in
which he had been himself educated, and to which
during his whole life he was a dedicated thing.[1]

——According to the faculty, or source, from
which the pleasure given by any poem or passage
was derived, I estimated the merit of such poem
or passage.   As the result of all my reading and
meditation, I abstracted two critical aphorisms,
deeming them to comprise the conditions and
criteria of poetic style; first, that not the poem
which we have *read*, but that to which we *return*,
with the greatest pleasure, possesses the genuine

---

[1] Coleridge spoke elsewhere in other terms of this famous schoolmaster.   Lamb and Leigh Hunt were also in "Christ's Hospital,"
and have given their accounts of Mr. Boyer; Lamb in "Recollec-
tions of Christ's Hospital," where he speaks of him favorably, and
in "Christ's Hospital Five and Thirty Years Ago," where he
describes him grimly enough; as does Hunt, in his Autobiography.

power, and claims the name of *essential poetry.*
Second, that whatever lines can be translated into
other words of the same language without diminu-
tion of their significance, either in sense or association, or in any worthy feeling, are so far vicious in
their diction. Be it, however, observed, that I
excluded from the list of worthy feelings, the
pleasure derived from mere novelty, in the reader,
and the desire of exciting wonderment at his powers
in the author. Oftentimes since then, in perusing
French tragedies, I have fancied two marks of
admiration at the end of each line, as hieroglyphics
of the author's own admiration at his own clever-
ness. Our genuine admiration of a great poet is
a continuous *under-current* of feeling; it is everywhere present, but seldom anywhere as a separate
excitement. I was wont boldly to affirm that it
would be scarcely more difficult to push a stone
from the pyramids with the bare hand, than to alter
a word or the position of a word in Milton or
Shakspeare (in their most important works at least),
without making the author say something else, or
something worse than he does say. One great distinction I appeared to myself to see plainly between
even the characteristic faults of our elder poets, and
the false beauty of the moderns. In the former,
from Donne to Cowley, we find the most fantastic
out-of-the-way thoughts, but in the most pure and
genuine mother English; in the latter, the most
obvious thoughts in language the most fantastic and
arbitrary. Our faulty elder poets sacrificed the

passion and passionate flow of poetry to the sub-
tleties of intellect, and to the starts of wit; the
moderns to the glare and glitter of a perpetual yet
broken and heterogeneous imagery, or rather to an
amphibious something, made up half of image and
half of abstract meaning. The one sacrificed the
heart to the head, the other both heart and head to
point and drapery.

From the Biographia Literaria. Chapter XIV.

During the first year that Mr. Wordsworth and I
were neighbors, our conversation turned frequently
on the two cardinal points of poetry, the power of
exciting the sympathy of the reader by a faithful ad·
herence to the truth of nature, and the power of giving the interest of novelty, by the modifying colors
of imagination. The sudden charm, which accidents
of light and shade, which moonlight or sunset, diffused over a known and familiar landscape, appeared
to represent the practicability of combining both.
These are the poetry of nature. The thought suggested itself (to which of us I do not recollect), that
a series of poems might be composed of two sorts.
In the one, the incidents and agents were to be, in
part at least, supernatural; and the excellence aimed
at, was to consist in the interesting of the affections
by the dramatic truth of such emotions, as would
naturally accompany such situations, supposing them
real. And real in *this* sense they have been to every
human being who, from whatever source of delusion,
has at any time believed himself under supernatural

agency. For the second class, subjects were to be chosen from ordinary life; the characters and incidents were to be such as will be found in every village and its vicinity, where there is a meditative and feeling mind to seek after them, or to notice them, when they present themselves.

In this idea originated the plan of the "Lyrical Ballads;" in which it was agreed that my endeavors should be directed to persons and characters supernatural, or at least romantic; yet so as to transfer from our inward nature a human interest, and a semblance of truth sufficient to procure for these shadows of imagination that willing suspension of disbelief for the moment, which constitutes poetic faith. Mr. Wordsworth, on the other hand, was to propose to himself, as his object, to give the charm of novelty to things of every day, and to excite a feeling analogous to the supernatural, by awakening the mind's attention from the lethargy of custom, and directing it to the loveliness and the wonders of the world before us; an inexhaustible treasure, but for which, in consequence of the film of familiarity and selfish solicitude, we have eyes, yet see not, ears that hear not, and hearts that neither feel nor understand.

With this view I wrote the "Ancient Mariner," and was preparing, among other poems, the "Dark Ladie," and the "Christabel," in which I should have more nearly realized my ideal than I had done in my first attempt. But Mr. Wordsworth's industry had proved so much more successful, and the

number of his poems so much greater, that my compositions, instead of forming a balance, appeared
rather an interpolation of heterogeneous matter.
Mr. Wordsworth added two or three poems written
in his own character, in the impassioned, lofty, and
sustained diction, which is characteristic of his
genius. In this form the "Lyrical Ballads" were
published ; and were presented by him, as an *experiment* whether subjects which, from their nature,
rejected the usual ornaments and extra-colloquial
style of poems in general, might not be so managed
in the language of ordinary life as to produce the
pleasurable interest which it is the peculiar business
of poetry to impart. To the second edition he
added a preface of considerable length ; in which,
notwithstanding some passages of apparently a contrary import, he was understood to contend for the
extension of this style to poetry of all kinds, and to
reject as vicious and indefensible all phrases and
forms of style that were not included in what he
(unfortunately, I think, adopting an equivocal expression) called the language of *real* life. From
this preface, prefixed to poems in which it was impossible to deny the presence of original genius,
however mistaken its direction might be deemed,
arose the whole long-continued controversy. For
from the conjunction of perceived power with supposed heresy I explain the inveteracy, and in some
instances, I grieve to say, the acrimonious passions,
with which the controversy has been conducted by
the assailants.

Had Mr. Wordsworth's poems been the silly, the childish things, which they were for a long time described as being ; had they been really distinguished from the compositions of other poets merely by meanness of language and inanity of thought ; had they, indeed, contained nothing more than what is found in the parodies, and pretended imitations of them,—they must have sunk at once, a dead weight, into the slough of oblivion, and have dragged the preface along with them. But year after year increased the number of Mr. Wordsworth's admirers. They were found, too, not in the lower classes of the reading public, but chiefly among young men of strong sensibility and meditative minds ; and their admiration (inflamed, perhaps, in some degree by opposition) was distinguished by its intensity, I might almost say by its *religious* fervor. These facts, and the intellectual energy of the author, which was more or less consciously felt, where it was outwardly and even boisterously denied; meeting with sentiments of aversion to his opinions, and of alarm at their consequences, produced an eddy of criticism which would of itself have borne up the poems by the violence with which it whirled them round and round. With many parts of this preface, in the sense attributed to them, and which the words undoubtedly seem to authorize, I never concurred ; but, on the contrary, objected to them as erroneous in principle, and as contradictory (in appearance at least) both to other parts of the same preface, and to the author's own practice in the greater number of the poems themselves. Mr. Wordsworth, in his recent collection, has, I find, degraded this prefatory disquisition to the end of his second volume, to be read or not at the reader's choice. But he has not, as far as I can discover, announced any change in his poetic creed. At all events, considering it as the source of a controversy in which I have been honored more than I deserve by the frequent conjunction of my name with his, I think it expedient to declare, once for all, in what points I coincide with his opinions, and in what points I altogether differ. But in order to render myself intelligible, I must previously, in as few words as possible, explain my ideas, first, of a POEM; and secondly, of POETRY itself, in *kind*, and in *essence*.

The office of philosophical *disquisition* consists in just *distinction;* while it is the privilege of the philosopher to preserve himself constantly aware that distinction is not division. In order to obtain adequate notions of any truth, we must intellectually separate its distinguishable parts; and this is the technical *process* of philosophy. But having so done, we must then restore them in our conceptions to the unity in which they actually coexist; and this is the *result* of philosophy. A poem contains the same elements as a prose composition; the difference, therefore, must consist in a different combination of them, in consequence of a different object proposed. Acccording to the difference of the object will be the difference of the combination. It is possible that the object may be

merely to facilitate the recollection of any given
facts or observations, by artificial arrangement; and
the composition will be a poem, merely because it is
distinguished from prose by metre, or by rhyme, or
by both conjointly.   In this, the lowest sense, a
man might attribute the name of a poem to the
well-known enumeration of the days in the several
months:

> "Thirty days hath September,
> April, June, and November," etc.,

and others of the same class and purpose.   And as
a particular pleasure is found in anticipating the recurrence of sounds and quantities, all compositions
that have this charm superadded, whatever be their
contents, *may* be entitled poems.

So much for the superficial *form*.   A difference of
objects and contents supplies an additional ground
of distinction.   The immediate purpose may be the
communication of truths; either of truth absolute
and demonstrable, as in works of science; or of facts
experienced and recorded, as in history.   Pleasure,
and that of the highest and most permanent kind,
may *result* from the *attainment* of the end; but it is
not itself the immediate end.   In other works the
communication of pleasure may be the immediate
purpose; and though truth, either moral or intellec·
tual, ought to be the *ultimate* end, yet this will dis·
tinguish the character of the author, not the class to
which the work belongs.   Blest, indeed, is that state
of society in which the immediate purpose would be

baffled by the perversion of the proper ultimate end ; in which no charm of diction or imagery could exempt the Bathyllus even of an Anacreon, or the Alexis of Virgil, from disgust and aversion !

But the communication of pleasure may be the immediate object of a work not metrically composed ; and that object may have been in a high degree attained, as in novels and romances. Would then the mere superaddition of metre, with or without rhyme, entitle *these* to the name of poems? The answer is, that nothing can permanently please, which does not contain in itself the reason why it is so, and not otherwise. If metre be superadded, all other parts must be made consonant with it. They must be such as to justify the perpetual and distinct attention to each part, which an exact correspondent recurrence of accent and sound is calculated to excite. The final definition, then, so deduced, may be thus worded : A poem is that species of composition which is opposed to works of science by proposing for its *immediate* object pleasure, not truth ; and from all other species (having *this* object in common with it) it is discriminated by proposing to itself such delight from the *whole*, as is compatible with a distinct gratification from each component *part.*

——Finally, GOOD SENSE is the BODY of poetic genius, FANCY its DRAPERY, MOTION its LIFE, and IMAGINATION the SOUL, that is everywhere, and in each ; and forms all into one graceful and intelligent whole.

From the Biographia Literaria. Chapter XV.

In the application of these principles to purposes of practical criticism, as employed in the appraisal of works more or less imperfect, I have endeavored to discover what the qualities in a poem are, which may be deemed promises and specific symptoms of poetic power, as distinguished from general talent determined to poetic composition by accidental motives, by an act of the will, rather than by the inspiration of a genial and productive nature. In this investigation I could not, I thought, do better than keep before me the earliest work of the greatest genius that, perhaps, human nature has yet produced, our *myriad-minded* Shakspeare. I mean the " Venus and Adonis," and the " Lucrece ; " works which give at once strong promises of the strength, and yet obvious proofs of the immaturity, of his genius. From these I abstracted the following marks, as characteristics of original poetic genius in general :

1. In the " Venus and Adonis " the first and most obvious excellence is the perfect sweetness of the versification ; its adaptation to the subject ; and the power displayed in varying the march of the words without passing into a loftier and more majestic rhythm than was demanded by the thoughts, or permitted by the propriety of preserving a sense of melody predominant. The delight in richness and sweetness of sound, even to a faulty excess, if it be evidently original, and not the result of an easily imitable mechanism, I regard as a highly favorable promise in the compositions of a young man. " The

man that hath not music in his soul " can, indeed,
never be a genuine poet.   Imagery (even taken from
nature, much more when transplanted from books, as
travels, voyages, and works of natural history) affecting incidents; just thoughts; interesting personal or
domestic feelings; and with these the art of their
combination or intertexture in the form of a poem,—
may all, by incessant effort, be acquired as a trade,
by a man of talents and much reading, who, as I
once before observed, has mistaken an intense desire
of poetic reputation for a natural poetic genius ; the
love of the arbitrary end for a possession of the peculiar means.   But the sense of musical delight, with
the power of producing it, is a gift of imagination ;
and this, together with the power of reducing multitude into unity of effect, and modifying a series of
thoughts by some one predominant thought or feeling, may be cultivated and improved, but can never
be learnt.   It is in these that " Poeta nascitur non
fit."

2. A second promise of genius is the choice of
subjects very remote from the private interests and
circumstances of the writer himself.   At least I have
found, that where the subject is taken immediately
from the author's personal sensations and experiences, the excellence of a particular poem is but an
equivocal mark, and often a fallacious pledge, of
genuine poetic power.   We may, perhaps, remember
the tale of the statuary who had acquired considerable reputation for the legs of his goddess, though
the rest of the statue accorded but indifferently

with the ideal beauty, till his wife, elated with the
husband's praises, modestly acknowledged that she
herself had been his constant model. In the Venus
and Adonis this proof of poetic power exists even
to excess. It is throughout as if a superior spirit,
more intuitive, more intimately conscious, even than
the characters themselves, not only of every outward
look and act, but of the flux and reflux of the mind
in all its subtlest thoughts and feelings, were placing the whole before our view ; himself, meanwhile,
unparticipating in the passions, and actuated only
by that pleasurable excitement, which had resulted
from the energetic fervor of his own spirit, in so
vividly exhibiting what it had so accurately and
profoundly contemplated. I think I should have
conjectured from these poems, that even the great
instinct which impelled the poet to the drama was
secretly working in him, prompting him by a series
and never-broken chain of imagery, always vivid,
and because unbroken, often minute ; by the highest effort of the picturesque in words, of which
words are capable, higher, perhaps, than was ever
realized by any other poet, even Dante not excepted ;
to provide a substitute for that visual language, that
constant intervention and running comment, by
tone, look, and gesture, which in his dramatic works
he was entitled to expect from the players. His
" Venus and Adonis " seem at once the characters
themselves, and the whole representation of those
characters by the most consummate actors. You seem
to be *told* nothing, but to see and hear everything.

Hence it is that from the perpetual activity óf attention required on the part of the reader; from the
rapid flow, the quick change, and the playful nature
of the thoughts and images ; and, above all, from
the alienation, and, if I may hazard such an expression, the utter *aloofness* of the poet's own feelings,
from those of which he is at once the painter and
the analyst,—that though the very subject cannot
but detract from the pleasure of a delicate mind, yet
never was poem less dangerous on a moral account.
Instead of doing as Ariosto, and as, still more offen-
sively, Weiland has done ; instead of degrading and
deforming passion into appetite, the trials of love
into the struggles of concupiscence, Shakspeare has
here represented the animal impulse itself, so as to
preclude all sympathy with it, by dissipating the
reader's notice among the thousand outward images,
and now beautiful, now fanciful, circumstances which
form its dresses and its scenery ; or by diverting our
attention from the main subject by those frequent
witty or profound reflections, which the poet's ever
active mind has deduced from, or connected with,
the imagery and the incidents. The reader is forced
into too much action to sympathize with the merely
passive of our nature. As little can a mind thus
roused and awakened be brooded on by mean and
indistinct emotion, as the low, lazy mist can creep
upon the surface of a lake, while a strong gale is
driving it onward in waves and billows.

3. It has been before observed, that images, however beautiful, though faithfully copied from nature,

and as accurately represented in words, do not of themselves characterize the poet. They become proofs of original genius, only as far as they are modified by a predominant passion ; or by associated thoughts or images awakened by that passion ; or, when they have the effect of reducing multitude to unity, or succession to an instant ; or, lastly, when a human and intellectual life is transferred to them from the poet's own spirit,

> " Which shoots its being through earth, sea, and air."

In the two following lines, for instance, there is nothing objectionable, nothing which would preclude them from forming, in their proper place, part of a descriptive poem :

> " Behold yon row of pines, that, shorn and bow'd,
> Bend from the sea-blast, seen at twilight eve."

But with the small alteration of rhythm the same words would be equally in their place in a book of topography or in a descriptive tour. The same image will rise into a semblance of poetry if thus conveyed :

> " Yon row of bleak and visionary pines,
> By twilight-glimpse discerned, mark ! how they flee
> From the fierce sea-blast, all their tresses wild
> Streaming before them."

I have given this as an illustration, by no means as an instance of that particular excellence which I had in view, and in which Shakespeare, even in his earliest, as in his latest works, surpasses all other poets. It is by this that he still gives a dignity and

a passion to the objects which he presents. Unaided
by any previous excitement, they burst upon us at
once in life and in power.

> " Full many a glorious morning have I seen
> *Flatter* the mountain tops with sovereign eye."
>
> *Shakespeare's Sonnet* 33.

> " Not mine own fears, nor the prophetic soul
> Of the wide world dreaming on things to come—
>
> . . . .
>
> The mortal moon hath her eclipse endured,
> And the sad augurs mock their own presage ;
> Incertainties now crown themselves assured,
> And peace proclaims olives of endless age.
> Now with the drops of this most balmy time
> My love looks fresh : and *Death* to me subscribes !
> Since spite of him I'll live in this poor rhyme,
> While he insults o'er dull and speechless tribes.
> And thou in this shalt find thy monument,
> When tyrants' crests and tombs of brass are spent."
>
> *Sonnet* 107.

As of higher worth, so doubtless still more characteristic of poetic genius does the imagery become
when it moulds and colors itself to the circumstances,
passion, or character present and foremost in the
mind. For unrivalled instances in this excellence
the reader's own memory will refer him to the Lear,
Othello, in short, to which not of the " great, ever-
living, dead man's" dramatic works? *Inopem me
copia fecit.* How true it is to nature, he has himself.
finely expressed in the instance of love, in Sonnet 98.

> " From you have I been absent in the spring,
> When proud pied April, drest in all its trim,
> Hath put a spirit of youth in every thing ;
> That heavy Saturn laugh'd and leap'd with him.

Yet nor the lays of birds, nor the sweet smell
Of different flowers in odor and in hue,
Could make me any summer's story tell,
Or from their proud lap pluck them, where they grew ;
Nor did I wonder at the lilies white,
Nor praise the deep vermilion in the rose ;
They were, tho' sweet, but figures of delight,
Drawn after you, you pattern of all those.
Yet seem'd it winter still, and you away,
As with your shadow I with these did play !

Scarcely less sure, or if a less valuable, not less indispensable mark will the image supply, when, with more than the power of the painter, the poet gives us the liveliest image of succession with the feeling of simultaneousness !

With this he breaketh from the sweet embrace
Of those fair arms, that held him to her heart,
And homeward through the dark lawns runs apace :
Look how a bright star shooteth from the sky !
So glides he through the night from Venus' eye.

4. The last character I shall mention, which would prove indeed but little, except as taken conjointly with the former, yet without which the former could scarce exist in a high degree, and (even if this were possible) would give promises only of transitory flashes and a meteoric power, is DEPTH, and ENERGY of THOUGHT. No man was ever yet a great poet without being at the same time a profound philosopher. For poetry is the blossom and the fragrancy of all human knowledge, human thoughts, human passions, emotions, language. In Shakespeare's *poems* the creative power and the intellectual energy

wrestle as in a war embrace.   Each in its excess of
strength seems to threaten the extinction of the other.
At length in the Drama they were reconciled, and
fought each with its shield before the breast of the
other.   Or, like two rapid streams, that at their first
meeting within narrow and rocky banks, mutually
strive to repel each other, and intermix reluctantly
and in tumult; but soon finding a wider channel and
more yielding shores, blend, and dilate, and flow on
in one current and with one voice.   The Venus and
Adonis did not, perhaps, allow the display of the
deeper passions.   But the story of Lucretia seems to
favor, and even demand, their intensest workings.
And yet we find in *Shakspeare's* management of the
tale neither pathos nor any other *dramatic* quality.
There is the same minute and faithful imagery as in
the former poem, in the same vivid colors, inspirited
by the same impetuous vigor of thought, and diverg-
ing and contracting with the same activity of the
assimilative and of the modifying faculties; and with
a yet larger display, a yet wider range of knowledge and reflection ; and, lastly, with the same perfect dominion, often *domination*, over the whole
world of language.   What then shall we say? even
this : that Shakespeare, no mere child of nature; no
automaton of genius; no passive vehicle of inspiration possessed by the spirit, not possessing it,—first
studied patiently, meditated deeply, understood mi-
nutely, till knowledge, become habitual and intuitive,
wedded itself to his habitual feelings, and at length
gave birth to that stupendous power, by which he

stands alone, with no equal or second in his own class; to that power which seated him on one of the two glory-smitten summits of the poetic mountain, with Milton as his compeer, not rival. While the former darts himself forth, and passes into all the forms of human character and passion, the one Proteus of the fire and the flood; the other attracts all forms and things to himself, in the unity of his own IDEAL. All things and modes of action shape themselves anew in the being of Milton; while Shakespeare becomes all things, yet forever remaining himself. O what great men hast thou not produced, England! my country! truly indeed—

> Must *we* be free or die, who speak the tongue
> Which *Shakspeare* spake ; the faith and morals hold
> Which *Milton* held. In everything we are sprung
> Of earth's first blood, have titles manifold !
>
> *Wordsworth.*

I conclude, therefore, that the attempt is impracticable; and that, were it not impracticable, it would still be useless. For the very power of making the selection implies the previous possession of the language selected. Or where can the poet have lived? And by what rules could he direct his choice, which would not have enabled him to select and arrange his words by the light of his own judgment? We do not adopt the language of a class by the mere adoption of such words exclusively as that class would use, or at least understand; but, likewise, by following the *order* in which the words of such men are wont to succeed each other. Now, this order, in the intercourse of uneducated men, is distinguished from the diction of their superiors in knowledge and power, by the greater *disjunction* and *separation* in the component parts of that, whatever it be, which they wish to communicate. There is a want of that prospectiveness of mind, that *surview*, which enables a man to foresee the whole of what he is to convey, appertaining to any one point ; and by this means so to subordinate and arrange the different parts according to their relative importance, as to convey it at once, and as an organized whole.

Now I will take the first stanza on which I have chanced to open, in the Lyrical Ballads. It is one of the most simple and least peculiar in its language.

> "In distant countries I have been,
> And yet I have not often seen
> A healthy man, a man full grown,
> Weep in the public road alone.
> But such a one, on English ground,
> And in the broad highway, I met ;
> Along the broad highway he came,
> His cheeks with tears were wet.
> Sturdy he seem'd, though he was sad,
> And in his arms a lamb he had."

The words here are doubtless such as are current in all ranks of life ; and, of course, not less so in the hamlet and cottage than in the shop, manufactory, college, or palace. But is this the *order* in which the rustic would have placed the words? I am grievously deceived if the following less *compact*

mode of commencing the same tale be not a far
more faithful copy. " I have been in a many parts,
far and near, and I don't know that I ever saw
before, a man crying by himself in the public road ;
a grown man I mean, that was neither sick nor
hurt," etc., etc. But when I turn to the following
stanza in " The Thorn : "

> " At all times of the day and night,
>   This wretched woman thither goes,
>   And she is known to every star,
>   And every wind that blows :
>   And there beside the thorn she sits,
>   When the blue daylight's in the skies,
>   And when the whirlwind's on the hill,
>   Or frosty air is keen and still ;
>   And to herself she cries,
>   Oh misery ! Oh misery !
>   Oh woe is me ! Oh misery !"

And compare this with the language of ordinary
men, or with that which I can conceive at all likely
to proceed, in *real* life, from *such* a narrator as is
supposed in the note to the poem ; compare it either
in the succession of the images or of the sentences,
I am reminded of the sublime prayer and hymn of
praise which Milton, in opposition to an established
liturgy, presents as a fair *specimen* of common contemporary devotion, and such as we might expect
to hear from every self-inspired minister of a con-
venticle ! And I reflect with delight, how little a
mere theory, though of his own workmanship, inter-
feres with the processes of genuine imagination in

a man of true poetic genius, who possesses, as Mr. Wordsworth, if ever man did, most assuredly does possess,

"THE VISION AND THE FACULTY DIVINE."

One point, then, alone remains, but the most important; its examination having been, indeed, my chief inducement for the preceding inquisition, " *There neither is, nor can be any essential difference between the language of prose and metrical composition.*" Such is Mr. Wordsworth's assertion. Now, prose itself, at least, in all argumentative and consecutive works, differs, and ought to differ, from the language of conversation; even as reading ought to differ from talking. Unless, therefore, the difference denied be that of the mere *words*, as materials common to all styles of writing, and not of the *style* itself, in the universally admitted sense of the term, it might be naturally presumed that there must exist a still greater between the ordonnance of poetic composition, and that of prose, than is expected to distinguish prose from ordinary conversation.

There are not, indeed, examples wanting in the history of literature, of apparent paradoxes that have summoned the public wonder, as new and startling truths, but which, on examination, have shrunk into tame and harmless *truisms;* as the eyes of a cat, seen in the dark, have been mistaken for flames of fire. But Mr. Wordsworth is among the last men to whom a delusion of this kind would be attributed by any one who had enjoyed the slightest opportunity of understanding his mind and character. Where an objection has been anticipated by such an author as natural, his answer to it must needs be interpreted in some sense which either is, or has been, or is capable of being, controverted. My object, then, must be to discover some other meaning for the term "*essential difference*" in this place, exclusive of the indistinction and community of the words themselves. For whether there ought to exist a class of words in the English in any degree resembling the poetic dialect of the Greek and Italian, is a question of very subordinate importance. The number of such words would be small indeed in our language, and even in the Italian and Greek; they consist not so much of different words, as of slight differences in the *forms* of declining and conjugating the same words; forms, doubtless, which having been, at some period more or less remote, the common grammatic flexions of some tribe or province, had been accidentally appropriated to poetry by the general admiration of certain master intellects, the first established lights of inspiration, to whom that dialect happened to be native.

Essence, in its primary signification, means the principle of *individuation*, the inmost principle of the *possibility* of any thing, *as* that particular thing. It is equivalent to the *idea* of a thing, whenever we use the word idea with philosophic precision. Existence, on the other hand, is distinguished from

essence by the superinduction of *reality*. Thus we
speak of the essence and essential properties of a
circle; but we do not therefore assert that any
thing which really *exists* is mathematically circular.
Thus too, without any tautology, we contend for
the *existence* of the Supreme Being; that is, for a
reality corresponding to the idea. There is, next,
a *secondary* use of the word essence, in which it
signifies the point or ground of contradistinction
between two modifications of the same substance or
subject. Thus we should be allowed to say, that
the style of architecture of Westminster Abbey is
essentially different from that of Saint Paul, even
though both had been built with blocks cut into the
same form, and from the same quarry. Only in
this latter sense of the term must it have been
denied by Mr. Wordsworth (for in this sense alone is
it *affirmed* by the general opinion) that the language
of poetry (i.e., the formal construction or architecture of the words and phrases) is *essentially* different
from that of prose. Now the burthen of the proof
lies with the oppugner, not with the supporters of
the common belief. Mr. Wordsworth, in consequence, assigns, as the proof of his position, "that
not only the language of a large portion of every
good poem, even of the most elevated character,
must necessarily, except with reference to the metre,
in no respect differ from that of good prose; but
likewise that some of the most interesting parts of
the best poems will be strictly the language of prose,
when prose is well written. The truth of this asser-

tion might be demonstrated by innumerable passages
from almost all the poetical writings even of Milton
himself." He then quotes Gray's sonnet—

> " In vain to me the smiling mornings shine,
> And reddening Phœbus lifts his golden fire ;
> The birds in vain their amorous descant join,
> Or cheerful fields resume their green attire;
> These ears, alas! for other notes repine ;
> *A different object do these eyes require;*
> *My lonely anguish melts no heart but mine,*
> *And in my breast the imperfect joys expire !*
> Yet morning smiles, the busy race to cheer,
> And new-born pleasure brings to happier men:
> The fields to all their wonted tributes bear,
> To warm their little loves the birds complain.
> *I fruitless mourn to him that cannot hear,*
> *And weep the more, because I weep in vain ;"*

and adds the following remark : " It will easily be
perceived that the only part of this Sonnet which is
of any value is the lines printed in italics. It is
equally obvious, that except in the rhyme, and in
the use of the single word " fruitless " for fruitlessly,
which is so far a defect, the language of these lines
does in no respect differ from that of prose."

An idealist defending his system by the fact that
when asleep we often believe ourselves awake, was
well answered by his plain neighbor, " Ah, but when
awake do we ever believe ourselves asleep?" Things
identical must be convertible. The preceding passage seems to rest on a similar sophism. For the
question is not, whether there may not occur in
prose an order of words which would be equally
proper in a poem; nor whether there are not

beautiful lines and sentences of frequent occurrence
in good poems which would be equally becoming, as
well as beautiful, in good prose; for neither the one
or the other has ever been either denied or doubted
by any one. The true question must be, whether
there are not modes of expression, a *construction*,
and an *order* of sentences which are in their fit and
natural place in a serious prose composition, but
would be disproportionate and heterogeneous in
metrical poetry; and, *vice versa*, whether in the language of a serious poem there may not be an arrangement both of words and sentences, and a use and
selection of (what are called) *figures of speech*, both
as to their kind, their frequency, and their occasions,
which, on a subject of equal weight, would be vicious
and alien in correct and manly prose. I contend
that in both cases this unfitness of each for the
place of the other frequently will and ought to exist.

And, first, from the *origin* of metre. This I
would trace to the balance in the mind effected by
that spontaneous effort which strives to hold in
check the workings of passion. It might be easily
explained, likewise, in what manner this salutary
antagonism is assisted by the very state which it
counteracts, and how this balance of antagonists
became organized into *metre* (in the usual accepta-
tion of that term), by a supervening act of the will
and judgment, consciously, and for the foreseen purpose of pleasure. Assuming these principles as the
data of our argument, we deduce from them two
legitimate conditions, which the critic is entitled to

expect in every metrical work. First · that as the
elements of metre owe their existence to a state of
increased excitement, so the metre itself should be
accompanied by the natural language of excitement.
Secondly, that as these elements are formed into
metre *artificially*, by a *voluntary* act, with the design
and for the purpose of blending *delight* with emotion,
so the traces of present *volition* should, throughout
the metrical language, be proportionally discernible.
Now these two conditions must be reconciled and
co-present.   There must be, not only a partnership,
but a union ; an interpenetration of passion and will,
of *spontaneous* impulse and of *voluntary* purpose.
Again : this union can be manifested only in a frequency of forms and figures of speech (originally
the offspring of passion, but now the adopted children of power), greater than would be desired or
endured where the emotion is not voluntarily en-
couraged, and kept up for the sake of that pleasure
which such emotion, so tempered and mastered by
the will, is found capable of communicating.   It not
only dictates, but of itself tends to produce a more
frequent employment of picturesque and vivifying
language than would be natural in any other case
in which there did not exist, as there does in the
present, a previous and well understood, though
tacit, *compact* between the poet and his reader, that
the latter is entitled to expect, and the former
bound to supply, this species and degree of pleasurable excitement.   We may in some measure apply
to this union the answer of Polixenes, in the

Winter's Tale, to Perdita's neglect of the streaked gilly-flowers, because she had heard it said,

> " There is an art which in their piedness shares
>   With great creating nature.
>   *Pol.*   Say there be:
>   Yet nature is made better by no mean,
>   But nature makes that mean.   So ev'n that art,
>   Which you say adds to nature, is an art
>   That nature makes !   You see, sweet maid, we marry
>   *A gentler scion to the wildest stock :*
>   And make conceive a bark of ruder kind
>   By bud of nobler race.   This is an art,
>   Which does mend nature—change it rather ; but
>   The art itself is nature.''

Secondly, I argue from the EFFECTS of metre. As far as metre acts in and for itself, it tends to increase the vivacity and susceptibility both of the general feelings and of the attention.   This effect it produces by the continued excitement of surprise, and by the quick reciprocations of curiosity, still gratified and still re-excited, which are too slight, indeed, to be at any one moment objects of distinct consciousness, yet become considerable in their aggregate influence.   As a medicated atmosphere, or as wine, during animated conversation, they act powerfully though themselves unnoticed.   Where, therefore, correspondent food and appropriate matter are not provided for the attention and feelings, thus roused, there must needs be a disappointment felt ; like that of leaping in the dark from the last step of a staircase, when we had prepared our muscles for a leap of three or four.

The discussion on the powers of metre in the preface is highly ingenious, and touches at all points on truth. But I cannot find any statement of its powers considered abstractly and separately. On the contrary, Mr. Wordsworth seems always to estimate metre by the powers which it exerts during (and, as I think, in *consequence of*) its combination with other elements of poetry. Thus the previous difficulty is left unanswered, *what* the elements are with which it must be combined in order to produce its own effects to any pleasurable purpose. Double and trisyllable rhymes, indeed, form a lower species of wit, and attended to, exclusively for their own sake, may become a source of momentary amusement; as in poor Smart's distich to the Welsh 'Squire, who had promised him a hare:

> "Tell me, thou son of great Cadwallader,
> Hast sent the hare, or hast thou swallow'd her?"

But, for any *poetic* purposes, metre resembles (if the aptness of the simile may excuse its meanness) yeast, worthless or disagreeable by itself, but giving vivacity and spirit to the liquor with which it is proportionally combined. . . . .

Metre in itself is simply a stimulant of the attention, and therefore excites the question—Why is the attention to be thus stimulated? Now the question cannot be answered by the pleasure of the metre itself; for this we have shown to be *conditional*, and dependent on the appropriateness of the thoughts and expressions, to which the metrical form is super-

added. Neither can I conceive any other answer
that can be rationally given, short of this: I write in
metre, because I am about to use a language different from that of prose. Besides, where the language
is not such, how interesting soever the reflections
are that are capable of being drawn by a philosophic
mind from the thoughts or incidents of the poem,
the metre itself must often become feeble. Take
the three last stanzas of the Sailor's Mother, for instance. If I could for a moment abstract from the
effect produced on the author's feelings, as a man,
by the incident at the time of its real occurrence, I
would dare appeal to his own judgment, whether in
the *metre* itself he found a sufficient reason for *their*
being written *metrically?*

> " And thus continuing, she said,
>   I had a son, who many a day
>   Sailed on the seas; but he is dead;
>   In Denmark he was cast away:
>   And I have travelled far as Hull, to see
>   What clothes he might have left, or other property.

> " The bird and cage, they both were his;
>   'T was my son's bird; and neat and trim
>   He kept it; many voyages
>   This singing-bird hath gone with him:
>   When last he sailed he left the bird behind;
>   As it might be, perhaps, from bodings of his mind.

> " He to a fellow-lodger's care
>   Had left it to be watched and fed,
>   Till he came back again; and there
>   I found it when my son was dead;
>   And now, God help me for my little wit!
>   I trail it with me, sir ! he took so much delight in it."

If disproportioning the emphasis we read these stanzas so as to make the rhymes perceptible, even *trisyllable* rhymes could scarcely produce an equal sense of oddity and strangeness, as we feel here in finding *rhymes at all* in sentences so exclusively colloquial. I would further ask whether, but for that visionary state into which the figure of the woman and the susceptibility of his own genius had placed the poet's imagination (a state which spreads its influence and coloring over all that co-exists with the exciting cause, and in which

> " The simplest and the most familiar things
> Gain a strange power of spreading awe around them "),—

I would ask the poet whether he would not have felt an abrupt downfall in these verses from the preceding stanza ?—

> " The ancient spirit is not dead;
> Old times, thought I, are breathing there !
> Proud was I that my country bred
> Such strength, a dignity so fair !
> She begged an alms, like one in poor estate;
> I looked at her again, nor did my pride abate."

It must not be omitted, and is, besides, worthy of notice, that those stanzas furnish the only fair instance that I have been able to discover in all Mr. Wordsworth's writings, of an *actual* adoption, or true imitation, of the *real* and *very* language of *low and rustic life*, freed from provincialisms.

Thirdly, I deduce the position from all the causes elsewhere assigned, which render metre the proper

form of poetry, and poetry imperfect and defective
without metre. Metre, therefore, having been connected with *poetry* most often and by a peculiar
fitness, whatever else is combined with *metre* must,
though it be not itself *essentially* poetic, have nevertheless some property in common with poetry, as an
intermedium of affinity, a sort (if I may dare borrow
a well-known phrase from technical chemistry) of
mordaunt between it and the superadded metre.
Now, poetry, Mr. Wordsworth truly affirms, does
always imply Passion, which word must be here
understood in its most general sense, as an excited
state of the feelings and faculties. And as every
passion has its proper' pulse, so will it likewise have
its characteristic modes of expression. But where
there exists that degree of genius and talent which
entitles a writer to aim at the honors of a poet, the
very *act* of poetic composition *itself* is, and is *allowed*
to imply and to produce, an unusual state of excitement, which, of course, justifies and demands a correspondent difference of language, as truly, though
not perhaps in as marked a degree, as the excitement of love, fear, rage, or jealousy. The vividness
of the description or declamations in Donne or
Dryden is as much and as often derived from the
force and fervor of the describer, as from the reflections, forms, or incidents which constitute their subject and materials. The wheels take fire from the
mere rapidity of their motion. To what extent,
and under what modifications, this may be admitted
to act, I shall attempt to define in an after remark

on Mr. Wordsworth's reply to this objection, or
rather on his objection to this reply, as already anticipated in his preface.

Fourthly, and as intimately connected with this,
if not the same argument in a more general form, I
adduce the high spiritual instinct of the human being,
impelling us to seek unity by harmonious adjustment, and thus establishing the principle, that *all*
the parts of an organized whole must be assimilated
to the more *important* and *essential* parts. This and
the preceding arguments may be strengthened by
the reflection, that the composition of a poem is
among the *imitative* arts, and that imitation, as opposed to copying, consists either in the interfusion
of the same, throughout the radically different, or
of the different throughout a base radically the
same.

Lastly, I appeal to the practice of the best poets
of all countries and in all ages, as *authorizing* the
opinion (*deduced* from all the foregoing), that in
every import of the word essential, which would
not here involve a mere truism, there may be, is,
and ought to be an *essential* difference between the
language of prose and of metrical composition.

In Mr. Wordsworth's criticism of Gray's Sonnet,
the reader's sympathy with his praise or blame of
the different parts is taken for granted, rather perhaps too easily. He has not, at least, attempted to
win or compel it by argumentative analysis. In *my*
conception, at least, the lines rejected as of no value
do, with the exception of the two first, differ as

much and as little from the language of common life as those which he has printed in italics as possessing genuine excellence. Of the five lines thus honorably distinguished, two of them differ from prose even more widely than the lines which either precede or follow, in the *position* of the words:

> " *A different object do these eyes require ;*
> My lonely anguish melts no heart but mine;
> *And in my breast the imperfect joys expire."*

But were it otherwise, what would this prove, but a truth, of which no man ever doubted? videlicet, that there are sentences which would be equally in their place both in verse and prose. Assuredly, it does not prove the point, which alone requires proof, namely, that there are not passages which would suit the one and not suit the other. The first line of this sonnet is distinguished from the ordinary language of men by the epithet to morning. (For we will set aside, at present, the consideration that the particular word "*smiling*" is hackneyed, and—as it involves a sort of personification—not quite congruous with the common and material attribute of *shining*.) And, doubtless, this adjunction of epithets, for the purpose of additional description, where no particular attention is demanded for the quality of the thing, would be noticed as giving a poetic cast to a man's conversation. Should the sportsman exclaim, " *Come, boys! the rosy morn calls you up,*" he will be supposed to have some song in his head. But no one suspects this when he says, "A wet morning shall not confine us to our beds." This, then, is either a defect in poetry, or it is not. Whoever should decide in the *affirmative*, I would request him to re-peruse any one poem, of any confessedly great poet, from Homer to Milton, or from Æschylus to Shakspeare, and to strike out (in thought I mean) every instance of this kind. If the number of these fancied erasures did not startle him, or if he continued to deem the work improved by their total omission, he must advance reasons of no ordinary strength and evidence—reasons grounded in the essence of human nature; otherwise I should not hesitate to consider him as a man not so much *proof against* all authority, as *dead* to it. The second line,

" And reddening Phœbus lifts his golden fire,"

has indeed almost as many faults as words. But then it is a bad line, not because the language is distinct from that of prose, but because it conveys incongruous images; because it confounds the cause and the effect, the real *thing* with the personified *representative* of the thing; in short, because it differs from the language of GOOD SENSE! That the " Phœbus" is hackneyed, and a school-boy image, is an *accidental* fault, dependent on the age in which the author wrote, and not deduced from the nature of the thing. That it is part of an exploded mythology, is an objection more deeply grounded. Yet when the torch of ancient learning was rekindled, so cheering were its beams, that our eldest poets, cut off by Christianity from all *accredited* machinery, and deprived of all *acknowledged* guardians and symbols of the great objects of nature, were naturally induced to adopt, as a *poetic* language, those fabulous personages, those forms of the supernatural in nature, which had given them such dear delight in the poems of their great masters. Nay, even at this day, what scholar of genial taste will not so far sympathize with them, as to read with pleasure in Petrarch, Chaucer, or Spenser what he would perhaps condemn as puerile in a modern poet?

CHARLES LAMB.

1775-1834.

[The most charming of all English essayists was also a fine
and sensitive critic. Lamb's short comments on Elizabethan
poets are famous, especially those in his volume of dramatic
selections. Here and there also in his essays we come upon
scraps of criticism, the best of them too occasional and dis-
connected to be introduced here. His own verse is pleasant,
not great; but in his prose the genuine and deep poetic note
of the man is everywhere audible. When his mood is
touched by an author, he has a strange art of making us
feel what is there, by some phrase which interprets to our
sensibilities even more than to our formal intelligence. In
style, thought, and emotion Lamb is one of the original
and creative writers of the century; and to be fond of his
essays is one of the clearest proofs of a refined literary taste.
He wrote but few pieces of systematic criticism. The first
of the two selections that follow is from one of these, "On
the Tragedies of Shakspere," a characteristically whimsical
special pleading against seeing them on the stage, a pleading
in which he himself perhaps only half believed. Two or
three passages in the essay are written superbly, as this par-
garaph upon Lear. The second selection is from the delightful essay "On Some of the Old Actors." Like much of Lamb's
work, his thought here is affected by a poetical caprice that
only partially investigates, for example, the steward's impulse
in tossing the ring upon the ground,—and that leaves us with
a one-sided impression. The sketch remains, however, one
of the most admirable fragments of Shaksperian criticism

that we possess. The hard, matter-of-fact side we can see for ourselves: what we welcome is the writing that makes us sympathize. If we are forced to an alternative between a cold pragmatic accuracy in the appreciation of Malvolio, or any other figure in poetry, and a realization of the finer essence of the character, its hidden secrets, we might do well to choose the latter. But we are much less likely to miss the truthful fact after we have felt the truthful soul.]

From the Essay on the Fitness of Shakespeare's Plays for Representation.

SO to see Lear acted—to see an old man tottering about the stage with a walking-stick, turned out of doors by his daughters in a rainy night—has nothing in it but what is painful and disgusting. We want to take him into shelter and relieve him. That is all the feeling which the acting of Lear ever produced in me. But the Lear of Shakspere cannot be acted. The contemptible machinery by which they mimic the storm which he goes out in, is not more inadequate to represent the horrors of the real elements, than any actor can be to represent Lear: they might more easily propose to personate the Satan of Milton upon a stage, or one of Michael Angelo's terrible figures. The greatness of Lear is not in corporal dimensions, but in intellectual: the explosions of his passion are terrible as a volcano: they are storms turning up and disclosing to the bottom that sea, his mind, with all its vast riches. It is his mind which is laid bare. This case of flesh and blood seems too insignificant to be thought on; even as he himself neglects it. On the stage we see nothing but corporal infirmities and weakness, the impotence of rage; while we read it, we see not Lear, but we are Lear—we are in his mind, we are sustained by a grandeur which baffles the malice of daughters and storms: in the aberrations of his reason we discover a mighty irregular power of reasoning immethodized from the ordinary purposes of life, but exerting its powers, as the wind blows where it listeth, at will upon the corruptions and abuses of mankind. What have looks or tones to do with that sublime identification of his age with that of the *heavens themselves*, when, in his reproaches to them for conniving at the injustice of his children, he reminds them that "they themselves are old"? What gestures shall we appropriate to this? What has the voice or the eye to do with such things? But the play is beyond all art, as the tamperings with it show: it is too hard and stony; it must have love-scenes, and a happy ending. It is not enough that Cordelia is a daughter: she must shine as a lover too. Tate has put his hook in the nostrils of this Leviathan, for Garrick and his followers, the showmen of the scene, to draw the mighty beast about more easily.

A happy ending! As if the living martyrdom that Lear had gone through—the flaying of his feelings alive—did not make a fair dismissal from the stage of life the only decorous thing for him. If he is to live and be happy after, if he could sustain this world's burden after, why all this pudder and preparation—why torment us with all this unnecessary sympathy? As if the childish pleasure of getting his gilt robes and sceptre again could tempt him to act over again his misused station—as if at his years, and with his experience, anything was left but to die.

From the Essays of Elia : on Some of the Old Actors.

Malvolio is not essentially ludicrous. He becomes comic but by accident. He is cold, austere, repelling; but dignified, consistent, and, for what appears, rather of an overstretched morality. Maria describes him as a sort of Puritan; and he might have worn his gold chain with honor in one of our old roundhead families, in the service of a Lambert or a Lady Fairfax. But his morality and his manners are misplaced in Illyria. He is opposed to the proper *levities* of the piece, and falls in the unequal contest. Still his pride, or his gravity (call it which you will), is inherent, and native to the man, not mock or affected, which latter only are the fit objects to excite laughter. His quality is at the best unlovely, but neither buffoon nor contemptible. His bearing is lofty, a little above his station, but probably not much above his deserts. We see no reason why he should not have been brave, honorable, accomplished. His careless committal of the ring to the ground (which he was commissioned to restore to Cesario) bespeaks a generosity of birth and feeling. His dialect on all occasions is that of a gentleman and a man of education. We must not confound him with the eternal old, low steward of comedy. He is master of the household to a great princess,—a dignity probably conferred upon him for other respects than age or length of service. Olivia, at the first indication of his supposed madness, declares that she "would not have him miscarry for half of her dowry." Does this look as if the character was meant to appear little or insignificant? Once, indeed, she accuses him to his face— of what?—of being "sick of self-love,"—but with a gentleness and considerateness which could not have been, if she had not thought that this particular infirmity shaded some virtues. His rebuke to the knight and his sottish revellers is sensible and spirited; and when we take into consideration the unprotected condition of his mistress, and the strict regard with which her state of real or dissembled mourning would draw the eyes of the world upon her house affairs, Malvolio might feel the honor of the family in some sort in his keeping; as it appears not that Olivia had any more brothers or kinsmen to look to it,—for Sir Toby had dropped all such nice respects at the buttery-hatch. That Malvolio was meant to be represented as possessing estimable qualities, the expression of the Duke, in his anxiety to have him reconciled, almost infers: "Pursue him, and entreat him to a peace." Even in his abused state of chains and darkness a sort of greatness seems never to desert him. He argues highly and well with the supposed Sir Topas, and philosophizes

gallantly upon his straw.¹ There must have been
some shadow of worth about the man; he must
have been something more than a mere vapor—a
thing of straw, or Jack in office—before Fabian and
Maria could have ventured sending him upon a
courting errand to Olivia. There was some con-
sonancy (as he would say) in the undertaking, or the
jest would have been too bold even for that house
of misrule.

Bensley, accordingly, threw over the part an air
of Spanish loftiness. He looked, spake, and moved
like an old Castilian. He was starch, spruce, opin-
ionated, but his superstructure of pride seemed bot-
tomed upon a sense of worth. There was something
in it beyond the coxcomb. It was big and swelling,
but you could not be sure that it was hollow. You
might wish to see it taken down, but you felt that
it was upon an elevation. He was magnificent from
the outset; but when the decent sobrieties of the
character began to give way, and the poison of self-
love, in his conceit of the Countess's affection,
gradually to work, you would have thought that
the hero of La Mancha in person stood before you.
How he went smiling to himself! with what ineffable carelessness would he twirl his gold chain! what
a dream it was! you were infected with the illusion,

---

¹ *Clown.* What is the opinion of Pythagoras concerning wild
fowl?
Mal. That the soul of our grandam might haply inhabit a bird.
Clown. What thinkest thou of his opinion?
Mal. I think nobly of the soul, and no way approve of his opinion.

and did not wish that it should be removed! you
had no room for laughter! if an unseasonable reflection of morality obtruded itself, it was a deep sense
of the pitiable infirmity of man's nature, that can lay
him open to such frenzies,—but in truth you rather
admired than pitied the lunacy while it lasted,—you
felt that an hour of such mistake was worth an age
with the eyes open. Who would not wish to live
but for a day in the conceit of such a lady's love as
Olivia? Why, the Duke would have given his prin-
cipality but for a quarter of a minute, sleeping or
waking, to have been so deluded. The man seemed
to tread upon air, to taste manna, to walk with his
head in the clouds, to mate Hyperion. O! shake
not the castles of his pride,—endure yet for a sea-
son, bright moments of confidence,—" stand still, ye
watches of the element," that Malvolio may be still
in fancy fair Olivia's lord!—but fate and retribution
say no!—I hear the mischievous titter of Maria,—
the witty taunts of Sir Toby—the still more insup-
portable triumph of the foolish knight—the counter-
feit Sir Topas is unmasked—and " thus the whirligig
of time," as the true clown hath it, " brings in his
revenges." I confess that I never saw the catastro-
phe of this character, while Bensley played it, without a kind of tragic interest.

THOMAS DE QUINCEY.

1785-1859.

[De Quincey's talent lay more in narrative and imaginative writing than in literary criticism. He was too digressive and sensational, too much of a rhetorician, to rank with the greatest critics. His liveliness of fancy and the rapid play of his remarkable information, together with his verbal brilliancy, found their most congenial field in his extraordinary rambling sketches. But his knowledge of literature was so wide and sympathetic, and he had such genuine philosophical insight, that he stands well as a writer on literary topics. His best work in this field is to be found fragmentarily all through those numerous volumes which he composed after his late commencement as an author. The following extract from his short essay on Language will open up an important element in the enjoyment of belles-lettres to any who have not realized this conception of style.]

From the Essay on Language.

1. IT is certain that style, or (to speak by the most general expression) the management of language, ranks amongst the fine arts, and is able therefore to yield a separate intellectual pleasure quite apart from the interest of the subject treated. So far it is already one error to rate the value of style as if it were necessarily a dependent or subordinate thing. On the contrary, style has an absolute value, like the product of any other exquisite art, quite distinct from

the value of the subject about which it is employed, and irrelatively to the subject; precisely as the fine workmanship of Scopas the Greek, or of Cellini the Florentine, is equally valued by the connoisseur, whether embodied in bronze or marble, in an ivory or golden vase. But—

2. If we *do* submit to this narrow valuation of style, founded on the interest of the subject to which it is ministerial, still, even on that basis, we English commit a capital blunder, which the French earnestly and sincerely escape; for, assuming that the thoughts involve the primary interest, still it must make all the difference in the world to the success of those thoughts, whether they are treated in the way best fitted to expel the doubts or darkness that may have settled upon them; and secondly, in cases where the business is, not to establish new convictions, but to carry old convictions into operative life and power, whether they are treated in the way best fitted to rekindle in the mind a practical sense of their value. Style has two separate functions—first, to brighten the *intelligibility* of a subject which is obscure to the understanding; secondly, to regenerate the normal *power* and impressiveness of a subject which has become dormant to the sensibilities. Darkness gathers upon many a theme, sometimes from previous mistreatment, but oftener from original perplexities investing its very nature. Upon the style it is, if we take that word in its largest sense— upon the skill and art of the developer, that these perplexities greatly depend for their illumination.

Look, again, at the other class of cases, when the
difficulties are not for the understanding, but for the
practical sensibilities as applicable to the services of
life.   The subject, suppose, is already understood
sufficiently; but it is lifeless as a motive. It is not new
light that is to be communicated, but old torpor that
is to be dispersed.   The writer is not summoned to
convince, but to persuade.   Decaying lineaments are
to be retraced, and faded coloring to be refreshed.
Now, these offices of style are really not essentially
original *discovery* of truth.   He that to an old conviction, long since inoperative and dead, gives the
regeneration that carries it back into the heart as a
vital power of action; he, again, that by new light,
or by light trained to flow through a new channel,
reconciles to the understanding a truth which hither-
to had seemed dark or doubtful,—both these men
are really, *quoad* us that benefit by their services,
the *discoverers* of the truth.   Yet these results are
amongst the possible gifts of style.   Light to *see* the
road, power to *advance along it*—such being amongst
the promises and proper functions of style, it is a
capital error, under the idea of its ministeriality, to
undervalue this great organ of the advancing intellect—an organ which is equally important considered
as a tool for the culture and *popularization* of truth,
and also (if it had no use at all in that way) as a
mode *per se* of the beautiful, and a fountain of intellectual pleasure.   The vice of that appreciation,
which we English apply to style, lies in representing
it as a mere ornamental accident of written compo-

sition—a trivial embellishment, like the mouldings of furniture, the cornices of ceilings, or the arabesques of tea-urns. On the contrary, it is a product of art the rarest, subtlest, and most intellectual; and like other products of the fine arts, it is then finest when it is most eminently disinterested, that is, most conspicuously detached from gross palpable uses. Yet, in very many cases, it really *has* the obvious uses of that gross palpable order; as in the cases just noticed, when it gives light to the understanding, or power to the will, removing obscurities from one set · of truths, and into another circulating the life-blood of sensibility. In these cases, meantime, the style is contemplated as a thing separable from the thoughts; in fact, as the *dress* of the thoughts—a robe that may be laid aside at pleasure. But—

3. There arises a case entirely different, where style cannot be regarded as a *dress* or alien covering, but where style becomes the *incarnation* of the thoughts. The human body is not the dress or apparel of the human spirit : far more mysterious is the mode of their union. Call the two elements A and B : then it is impossible to point out A as existing aloof from B, or *vice versa.* A exists in and through B, B exists in and through A. No profound observer can have failed to observe this illustrated in the capacities of style. Imagery is sometimes not the mere alien apparelling of a thought, and of a nature to be detached from the thought, but is the coefficient that, being superadded to something else, absolutely *makes* the thought.

THOMAS CARLYLE.

1795–1881.

[Carlyle wrote frequently on literary topics, though more
from the intellectual than the æsthetic standpoint. Some of
his critical essays, notably that upon Burns, are among the
- best of their class.   His power of sympathy in itself makes
him a true critic, aside from his sharp insight and vivid expression. The quotations given below are from the Hero as
Man of Letters, one of the lectures in his popular volume
on Heroes and Hero-worship.   This analysis of the secrets
and tests of success in poetry is most suggestive.   The
sketch of Dante, while an exception to the manner of most
of our selections, is too characteristic of Carlyle and too
fine to be omitted from its context.]

**From the Lecture on " The Poet " in Heroes and Hero Wor-
ship.**

POET and prophet differ greatly in our loose modern notions of them.   In some old languages, again,
the titles are synonymous ; *Vates* means both prophet
and poet : and indeed at all times, prophet and poet,
well understood, have much kindred of meaning.
Fundamentally indeed they are the same ; in this
most important respect especially, that they have
penetrated both of them into the sacred mystery of
the universe ; what Goethe calls " the open secret."
" Which is the great secret ?" asks one.—" The *open*
secret,"—open to all, seen by almost none !   That

divine mystery, which lies everywhere in all beings,
"the divine idea of the world, that which lies at the
bottom of appearance," as Fichte styles it; of which
all appearance, from the starry sky to the grass of
the field, but especially the appearance of man and
his work, is but the *vesture*, the embodiment that
renders it visible. This divine mystery *is* in all
times and in all places ; veritably is. In most times
and places it is greatly overlooked; and the universe, definable always in one or the other dialect,
as the realized thought of God, is considered a
trivial, inert, commonplace matter,—as if, says the
satirist, it were a dead thing, which some uphol-
sterer had put together. It could do no good, at
present, to *speak* much about this; but it is a pity
for every one of us if we do not know it, live ever in
the knowledge of it. Really a most mournful pity ;
—a failure to live at all, if we live otherwise !
———But now, I say, whoever may forget this
divine mystery, the *Vates*, whether prophet or poet,
has penetrated into it ; is a man sent hither to make
it more impressively known to us. That always is his
message ; he is to reveal that to us,—that sacred mystery which he more than others lives ever present
with. While others forget it, he knows it ;—I might
say, he has been driven to know it ; without consent
asked of *him*, he finds himself living in it, bound
to live in it. Once more, here is no hearsay, but a
direct insight and belief ; this man too could not
help being a sincere man ! Whosoever may live in
the shows of things, it is for him a necessity of

nature to live in the very fact of things. A man once more, in earnest with the universe, though all others were but toying with it. He is a *Vates*, first of all, in virtue of being sincere. So far poet and prophet, participators in the "open secret," are one.

With respect to their distinction again: the *Vates* prophet, we may say, has seized that sacred mystery rather on the moral side, as good and evil, duty and prohibition; the *Vates* poet on what the Germans call the æsthetic side, as beautiful, and the like. The one we may call a revealer of what we are to do, the other of what we are to love. But indeed these two provinces run into one another, and cannot be disjoined. The prophet too has his eye on what we are to love: how else shall he know what it is we are to do? The highest voice ever heard on this earth said withal, "Consider the lilies of the field: they toil not, neither do they spin: yet Solomon in all his glory was not arrayed like one of these." A glance, that, into the deepest deep of beauty. "The lilies of the field,"—dressed finer than earthly princes, springing-up there in the humble furrow-field; a beautiful *eye* looking-out on you, from the great inner sea of beauty! How could the rude earth make these, if her essence, rugged as she looks and is, were not inwardly beauty? In this point of view, too, a saying of Goethe's, which has staggered several, may have meaning: "The beautiful," he intimates, "is higher than the good; the beautiful includes in it the good." The *true* beautiful; which however, I have said somewhere, "differs from the *false* as heaven does from Vauxhall!" So much for the distinction and identity of poet and prophet.—

In ancient and also in modern periods we find a few poets who are accounted perfect; whom it were a kind of treason to find fault with. This is noteworthy; this is right: yet in strictness it is only an illusion. At bottom, clearly enough, there is no perfect poet! A vein of poetry exists in the hearts of all men; no man is made altogether of poetry. We are all poets when we *read* a poem well. The "imagination that shudders at the Hell of Dante," is not that the same faculty, weaker in degree, as Dante's own? No one but Shakespeare can embody out of *Saxo Grammaticus*, the story of "Hamlet" as Shakespeare did: but every one models some kind of story out of it; every one embodies it better or worse. We need not spend time in defining. Where there is no specific difference, as between round and square, all definition must be more or less arbitrary. A man that has *so* much more of the poetic element developed in him as to become noticeable, will be called poet by his neighbors. World-poets too, those whom we are to take for perfect poets, are settled by critics in the same way. One who rises *so* far above the general level of poets will, to such and such critics, seem a universal poet; as he ought to do. And yet it is, and must be, an arbitrary distinction. All poets, all men, have some touches of the universal; no man is wholly made of that. Most poets are very soon forgotten: but not the noblest Shakespeare or Homer of them can be remembered *forever ;*—a day comes when he too is not!

Nevertheless, you will say, there must be a differ-ence between true poetry and true speech not poeti-cal: what is the difference? On this point many things have been written, especially by late German critics, some of which are not very intelligible at first. They say, for example, that the poet has an *infini-tude* in him ; communicates an *unendlichkeit*, a cer-tain character of "infinitude," to whatsoever he delineates. This, though not very precise, yet on so vague a matter is worth remembering: if well meditated, some meaning will gradually be found in it. For my own part, I find considerable meaning in the old vulgar distinction of poetry being *metrical*, having music in it, being a song. Truly, if pressed to give a definition, one might say this as soon as anything else: If your delineation be authentically *musical*, musical not in word only, but in heart and substance, in all the thoughts and utterances of it, in the whole conception of it, then it will be poetical ; if not, not.—Musical: how much lies in that ! A *musical* thought is one spoken by a mind that has penetrated into the inmost heart of the thing ; de-tected the inmost mystery of it, namely the *melody* that lies hidden in it ; the inward harmony of coher-ence, which is its soul, whereby it exists, and has a right to be, here in this world. All inmost things, we may say, are melodious ; naturally utter them-selves in song. The meaning of song goes deep. Who is there that, in logical words, can express the

effect music has on us? A kind of inarticulate
unfathomable speech, which leads us to the edge of
the infinite, and lets us for moments gaze into that!

Nay all speech, even the commonest speech, has
something of song in it: not a parish in the world
but has its parish accent;—the rhythm or *tune* to
which the people there *sing* what they have to say!
Accent is a kind of chanting; all men have accent
of their own,—though they only *notice* that of others.
Observe too how all passionate language does of
itself become musical,—with a finer music than the
mere accent; the speech of a man even in zealous
anger becomes a chant, a song. All deep things are
song. It seems somehow the very central essence
of us, song; as if all the rest were but wrappages
and hulls! The primal element of us; of us, and of
all things. The Greeks fabled of sphere-harmonies:
it was the feeling they had of the inner structure of
nature; that the soul of all her voices and utterance were perfect music. Poetry, therefore, we will
call *musical thought*. The poet is he who *thinks* in
that manner. At bottom, it turns still on power of
intellect; it is a man's sincerity and depth of vision
that makes him a poet. See deep enough, and you
see musically; the heart of nature *being* everywhere
music, if you can only reach it.

The *Vates* poet, with his melodious apocalypse of
nature, seems to hold a poor rank among us, in comparison with the *Vates* prophet; his function, and
our esteem of him for his function, alike slight. The
hero taken as divinity; the hero taken as prophet;

then next the hero taken only as poet: does it not look as if our estimate of the great man, epoch after epoch, were continually diminishing? We take him first for a god, then for one god-inspired ; and now in the next stage of it, his most miraculous word gains from us only the recognition that he is a poet, beautiful verse-maker, man of genius, or suchlike!— It looks so ; but I persuade myself that intrinsically it is not so. If we consider well, it will perhaps appear that in man there is the *same* altogether peculiar admiration for the heroic gift, by what name soever called, that there at any time was.

I should say, if we do not reckon a great man literally divine, it is that our notions of God, of the supreme unattainable fountain of splendor, wisdom and heroism, are ever rising *higher;* not altogether that our reverence for these qualities, as manifested in our like, is getting lower. This is worth taking thought of. Skeptical dilettantism, the curse of these ages, a curse which will not last forever, does indeed in this the highest province of human things, as in all provinces, make sad work ; and our reverence for great men, all crippled, blinded, paralytic as it is, comes out in poor plight, hardly recognizable. Men worship the shows of great men ; the most disbelieve that there is any reality of great men to worship. The dreariest, fatalest faith ; believing which, one would literally despair of human things. Nevertheless look, for example, at Napoleon! A Corsican lieutenant of artillery; that is the show of *him:* yet is he not obeyed, *worshipped* after his sort, as all the tiaraed and diademed of the world put together could not be? High duchesses, and ostlers of inns, gather round the Scottish rustic, Burns;—a strange feeling dwelling in each that they never heard a man like this; that, on the whole, this is the man! In the secret heart of these people it still dimly reveals itself, though there is no accredited way of uttering it at present, that this rustic, with his black brows and flashing sun-eyes, and strange words moving laughter and tears, is of a dignity far beyond all others, incommensurable with all others. Do not we feel it so? But now, were dilettantism, skepticism, triviality, and all that sorrowful brood, cast-out of us,—as, by God's blessing, they shall one day be; were faith in the shows of things entirely swept-out, replaced by clear faith in the *things*, so that a man acted on the impulse of that only, and counted the other non-extant, what a new livelier feeling towards this Burns were it!

Nay here in these ages, such as they are, have we not two mere poets, if not deified, yet we may say beautified? Shakespeare and Dante are saints of poetry; really, if we will think of it, *canonized*, so that it is impiety to meddle with them. The unguided instinct of the world, working across all these perverse impediments, has arrived at such result. Dante and Shakespeare are a peculiar two. They dwell apart, in a kind of royal solitude; none equal, none second to them; in the general feeling of the world, a certain transcendentalism, a glory as of complete perfection, invests these two. They *are* canonized, though no pope or cardinal took hand in doing it! Such, in spite of every perverting influence, in the most unheroic times, is still our indestructible reverence for heroism.

Many volumes have been written by way of commentary on Dante and his book; yet, on the whole, with no great result. His biography is, as it were, irrecoverably lost for us. An unimportant, wandering, sorrow-stricken man, not much note was taken of him while he lived; and the most of that has vanished, in the long space that now intervenes. It is five centuries since he ceased writing and living here. After all commentaries, the book itself is mainly what we know of him. The book;—and one might add that portrait commonly attributed to Giotto,[1] which, looking on it, you cannot help inclining to think genuine, whoever did it. To me it is a most touching face; perhaps of all faces that I know, the most so. Lonely there, painted as on vacancy, with the simple laurel wound round it; the deathless sorrow and pain, the known victory which is also deathless;—significant of the whole history of Dante! I think it is the mournfulest face that ever was painted from reality; an altogether tragic, heart-affecting face. There is in it, as foundation of it, the softness, tenderness, gentle affection as of a child; but all this is as if congealed into sharp

---

[1] [Giotto's portrait, published by the Arundel Society after Mr. Kirkup's tracing from the wall of the Podestá, represents Dante as young and placid.]

contradiction, into abnegation, isolation, proud hopeless pain. A soft ethereal soul looking-out so stern,
implacable, grim-trenchant, as from imprisonment
of thick-ribbed ice! Withal it is a silent pain too,
a silent scornful one: the lip is curled in a kind of
godlike disdain of the thing that is eating-out his
heart,—as if it were withal a mean insignificant
thing, as if he whom it had power to torture and
strangle were greater than it. The face of one
wholly in protest, and life-long unsurrendering battle,
against the world. Affection all converted into
indignation: an implacable indignation; slow, equa-
ble, silent, like that of a god! The eye too, it looks-
out as in a kind of *surprise*, a kind of inquiry, why
the world was of such a sort? This is Dante: so
he looks, this "voice of ten silent centuries," and
sings us " his mystic unfathomable song."

Perhaps one would say, *intensity*, with the much
that depends on it, is the prevailing character of
Dante's genius. Dante does not come before us as
a large catholic mind; rather as a narrow, and even
sectarian mind; it is partly the fruit of his age and
position, but partly too of his own nature. His
greatness has, in all senses, concentrated itself into
fiery emphasis and depth. He is world-great not
because he is world-wide, but because he is world-
deep. Through all objects he pierces as it were
down into the heart of being. I know nothing so
intense as Dante. Consider, for example, to begin
with the outermost development of his intensity,

consider how he paints. He has a great power of
vision ; seizes the very type of a thing ; presents
that and nothing more. You remember that first
view he gets of the Hall of Dite : *red* pinnacle, red-
hot cone of iron glowing through the dim immensity
of gloom; so vivid, so distinct, visible at once and
forever! It is an emblem of the whole genius of
Dante. There is a brevity, an abrupt precision in
him. Tacitus is not briefer, more condensed ; and
then in Dante it seems a natural condensation, spontaneous to the man. One smiting word ; and then
there is silence, nothing more said. His silence is
more eloquent than words. It is strange with what
a sharp decisive grace he snatches the true likeness
of a matter : cuts into the matter as with a pen of
fire. Plutus, the blustering giant, collapses at Virgil's rebuke ; it is " as the sails sink, the mast being
suddenly broken." Or that poor Brunetto Latini,
with the *cotto aspetto*, " face *baked*," parched, brown
and lean ; and the " fiery snow " that falls on them
there, a " fiery snow without wind," slow, deliberate,
never-ending ! Or the lids of those tombs ; square
sarcophaguses, in that silent dim-burning hall, each
with its soul in torment : the lids laid open there ;
they are to be shut at the day of judgment, through
eternity. And how Farinata rises; and how Caval-
cante falls—at hearing of his son, and the past tense
"*fue*"! The very movements in Dante have something brief ; swift, decisive, almost military. It is of
the inmost essence of his genius, this sort of painting. The fiery, swift Italian nature of the man, so

silent, passionate, with its quick abrupt movements, its silent " pale rages," speaks itself in these things.

.For though this of painting is one of the outermost developments of a man, it comes like all else from the essential faculty of him; it is physiognomical of the whole man. Find a man whose words paint you a likeness, you have found a man worth something; mark his manner of doing it, as very characteristic of him. In the first place, he could not have discerned the object at all, or seen the vital type of it, unless he had, what we may call, *sympathized* with it,—had sympathy in him to bestow on objects. He must have been *sincere* about it too; sincere and sympathetic: a man without worth cannot give you the likeness of any object; he dwells on vague outwardness, fallacy and trivial hearsay, about all objects. And indeed may we not say that intellect altogether expresses itself in this power of discerning what an object is? Whatsoever of faculty a man's mind may have will come out here. Is it even of business, a matter to be done? The gifted man is he who *sees* the essential point, and leaves all the rest aside as surplusage; it is his faculty too, the man of business's faculty, that he discern the true *likeness*, not the false superficial one, of the thing he has got to work in. And how much of *morality* is in the kind of insight we get of anything: "the eye seeing in all things what it brought with it the faculty of seeing!" To the mean eye all things are trivial, as certainly as to the jaundiced they are yellow. Raphael, the painters tell us, is the best of all portrait-painters withal. No most gifted eye can exhaust the significance of any object. In the commonest human face there lies more than Raphael will take-away with him.

Dante's painting is not graphic only, brief, true, and of a vividness as of fire in dark night; taken on the wider scale, it is every way noble, and the outcome of a great soul. Francesca[1] and her lover, what qualities in that! A thing woven as out of rainbows, on a ground of eternal black. A small flute-voice of infinite wail speaks there, into our very hearts of hearts. A touch of womanhood in it too: *della bella persona, che mi fu tolta;*[2] and how, even in the pit of woe, it is a solace that *he* will never part from her! Saddest tragedy in these *alti guai.*[3] And the racking winds, in that *aer bruno*, whirl them away again, to wail forever!—Strange to think: Dante was the friend of this poor Francesca's father; Francesca herself may have sat upon the poet's knee, as a bright innocent little child. Infinite pity, yet also infinite rigor of law: it is so nature is made; it is so Dante discerned that she was made. What a paltry notion is that of his "Divine Comedy's" being a poor splenetic impotent terrestrial libel; putting those into hell whom he could not be avenged-upon on earth! I suppose if ever pity, tender as a mother's, was in the heart of any man, it was in Dante's. But a man who does not

---

[1] [Inferno, 5.]

[2] [That human loveliness, which I have lost.]

[3] [Shrill cries of woe]

know rigor cannot pity, either. His very pity will
be cowardly, egoistic,—sentimentality, or little better. I know not in the world an affection equal to
that of Dante. It is a tenderness, a trembling, long-
ing, pitying love : like the wail of æolean harps, soft,
soft ; like a child's young heart ;—and then that
stern, sore-saddened heart ! These longings of his
towards his Beatrice ; their meeting together in the
Paradiso ; his gazing in her pure transfigured eyes,
her that had been purified by death so long, separated from him so far :—one likens it to the song of
angels ; it is among the purest utterances of affection, perhaps the very purest, that ever came out of
a human soul.

MATTHEW ARNOLD.

1822–1888.

[No other English author who has written both in verse and in prose has been so successful in each as Matthew Arnold. Some of the best judgments of the time count him among his country's most perfect poets, and recognize in his poems a chastened elegance and charm of language and a reflection of important phases of contemporaneous thought which they find nowhere else. The general public, however, knows him best by his prose. His expression imparts value even to his less interesting essays, and intimacy with his work cannot fail to cultivate one's feeling for style. His intellectual habit is mainly critical, and his reviews of society, literature, and certain contested topics of nineteenth-century belief are all marked by self-possession, urbanity, and the scrutiny of a trained and variously informed mind, which is restrained from hardness by the gift of poetic and sympathetic feeling. Possibly his attitude is too scrupulously correct, sometimes it may seem over severe and unbending in matters of taste. We may occasionally chafe at a certain superiority of tone which Sydney Smith remarked in his bearing while a young man, and certainly he entertains opinions which many cannot accept. It is not difficult to mention greater scholars and thinkers of his own day. But Arnold is the master of so rare a discrimination, such tact in selection, such certainty of touch in his own best field, such earnestness and strength despite his studied calm and the humor that plays over his pages, that we can scarcely overrate the service he has rendered to many in search of a conscientiously thoughtful intelligence, and a more refined and observant taste. As a literary critic he may profitably be compared with Sainte-Beuve, whom he admired warmly.]

From Celtic Literature.

——IF I were asked where English poetry got these three things,— its turn for style, its turn for melancholy, and its turn for natural magic, for catching and rendering the charm of nature in a wonderfully near and vivid way,—I should answer, with some doubt, that it got much of its turn for style from a Celtic source ; with less doubt, that it got much of its melancholy from a Celtic source ; with no doubt at all, that from a Celtic source it got nearly all its natural magic.

Any German with penetration and tact in matters of literary criticism will own that the principal deficiency of German poetry is in style ; that for style, in the highest sense, it shows but little feeling. Take the eminent masters of style, the poets who best give the idea of what the peculiar power which lies in style is,—Pindar, Virgil, Dante, Milton. An example of the peculiar effect which these poets produce, you can hardly give from German poetry. Examples enough you can give from German poetry of the effect produced by genius, thought, and feeling expressing themselves in clear language, simple language, passionate language, eloquent language, with harmony and melody ; but not of the peculiar effect exercised by eminent power of style. Every

reader of Dante can at once call to mind what the
peculiar effect I mean is ; I spoke of it in my lectures on translating Homer, and there I took an example of it from Dante, who perhaps manifests it
more eminently than any other poet.   But from
Milton, too, one may take examples of it abundantly ; compare this from Milton :

> . . . . . nor sometimes forget
> Those other two equal with me in fate,
> So were I equall'd with them in renown,
> Blind Thamyris and blind Mæonides—

with this from Goethe :

> Es bildet ein Talent sich in der Stille,
> Sich ein Character in dem Strom der Welt.

Nothing can be better in its way than the style in
which Goethe there presents his thought, but it is
the style of prose as much as of poetry ; it is lucid-
harmonious, earnest, eloquent, but it has not received
that peculiar kneading, heightening, and recasting
which is observable in the style of the passage from
Milton,—a style which seems to have for its cause a
certain pressure of emotion, and an ever-surging, yet
bridled, excitement in the poet, giving a special intensity to his way of delivering himself.   In poetical
races and epochs this turn for style is peculiarly
observable ; and perhaps it is only on condition of
having this somewhat heightened and difficult manner, so different from the plain manner of prose,
that poetry gets the privilege of being loosed, at its
best moments, into that perfectly simple, limpid

style, which is the supreme style of all, but the simplicity of which is still not the simplicity of prose. The simplicity of Menander's style is the simplicity of prose, and is the same kind of simplicity as that which Goethe's style, in the passage I have quoted, exhibits; but Menander does not belong to a great poetical moment, he comes too late for it ; it is the simple passages in poets like Pindar or Dante which are perfect, being masterpieces of *poetical* simplicity. One may say the same of the simple passages in Shakespeare; they are perfect, their simplicity being a *poetical* simplicity. They are the golden, easeful, crowning moments of a manner which is always pitched in another key from that of prose, a manner changed and heightened ; the Elizabethan style, regnant in most of our dramatic poetry to this day, is mainly the continuation of this manner of Shakespeare's. It was a manner much more turbid and strewn with blemishes than the manner of Pindar, Dante, or Milton; often it was detestable; but it owed its existence to Shakespeare's instinctive impulse towards *style* in poetry, to his native sense of the necessity for it ; and without the basis of style everywhere, faulty though it may in some places be, we should not have had the beauty of expression, unsurpassable for effectiveness and charm, which is reached in Shakespeare's best passages. The turn for style is perceptible all through English poetry, proving, to my mind, the genuine poetical gift of the race; this turn imparts to our poetry a stamp of high distinction, and sometimes it doubles the force

of a poet not by nature of the very highest order,
such as Gray, and raises him to a rank beyond what
his natural richness and power seem to promise.
Goethe, with his fine critical perception, saw clearly
enough both the power of style in itself, and the
lack of style in the literature of his own country;
and perhaps if we regard him solely as a German,
not as a European, his great work was that he
labored all his life to impart style into German literature, and firmly to establish it there.   Hence the
immense importance to him of the world of classical
art, and of the productions of Greek or Latin genius,
where style so eminently manifests its power.   Had
he found in the German genius and literature an
element of style existing by nature and ready to his
hand, half his work, one may say, would have been
saved him, and he might have done much more in
poetry.   But as it was, he had to try and create, out
of his own powers, a style for German poetry, as
well as to provide contents for this style to carry;
and thus his labor as a poet was doubled.

It is to be observed that power of style, in the
sense in which I am here speaking of style, is something quite different from the power of idiomatic,
simple, nervous, racy expression, such as the expression of healthy, robust natures so often is, such as
Luther's was in a striking degree.   Style, in my
sense of the word, is a peculiar recasting and heightening, under a certain condition of spiritual excitement, of what a man has to say, in such a manner
as to add dignity and distinction to it; and dignity

and distinction are not terms which suit many acts
or words of Luther. Deeply touched with the *Gemeinheit* which is the bane of his nation, as he is
at the same time a grand example of the honesty
which is his nation's excellence, he can seldom even
show himself brave, resolute, and truthful, without
showing a strong dash of coarseness and common-
ness all the while ; the right definition of Luther,
as of our own Bunyan, is that he is a Philistine of
genius. So Luther's sincere idiomatic German,—
such language is this : " Hilf lieber Gott, wie man-
chen Jammer habe ich gesehen, dass der gemeine
Mann doch so gar nichts weiss von der christlichen
Lehre !"—no more proves a power of style in German literature, than Cobbett's sinewy idiomatic
English proves it in English literature. Power of
style, properly so called, as manifested in masters
of style like Dante or Milton in poetry, Cicero, Bossuet or Bolingbroke in prose, is something quite different, and has, as I have said, for its characteristic
effect, this : to add dignity and distinction.

——There are many ways of handling nature, and
we are here only concerned with one of them ; but a
rough-and-ready critic imagines that it is all the same
so long as nature is handled at all, and fails to draw
the needful distinction between modes of handling
her. But these modes are many ; I will mention
four of them now : there is the conventional way of
handling nature, there is the faithful way of handling
nature, there is the Greek way of handling nature,
there is the magical way of handling nature. In all

these three last the eye is on the object, but with a
difference: in the faithful way of handling nature,
the eye is on the object, and that is all you can say;
in the Greek, the eye is on the object, but lightness
and brightness are added; in the magical, the eye is
on the object, but charm and magic are added.   In
the conventional way of handling nature, the eye is
not on the object; what that means we all know,
we have only to think of our eighteenth century
poetry—

     " As when the moon, refulgent lamp of night "—

to call up any number of instances.   Latin poetry
supplies plenty of instances too; if we put this from
Propertius's *Hylas*—

   . . .   "manus heroum . . . .
  Mollia composita litora fronde tegit "—

side by side the line of Theocritus by which it was
suggested—

"λειμων γαρ σφιν ἔκειτο μέγας, στιβάδεσσιν ονειαρ "—

we get at the same moment a good specimen both
of the conventional and of the Greek way of handling nature.   But from our own poetry we may get
specimens of the Greek way of handling nature, as
well as of the conventional: for instance, Keats's

    " What little town, by river or seashore,
      Or mountain-built with quiet citadel,
      Is emptied of its folk, this pious morn?"

is Greek, as Greek as a thing from Homer or Theocritus; it is composed with the eye on the object, a

radiancy and light clearness being added. German
poetry abounds in specimens of the faithful way of
handling nature ; an excellent example is to be found
in the stanzas called *Zueignung*,¹ prefixed to Goethe's
poems ; the morning walk, the mist, the dew, the
sun, are as faithful as they can be, they are given
with the eye on the object, but there the merit of the
work, as a handling of nature, stops ; neither Greek
radiance nor Celtic magic is added ; the power of
these is not what gives the poem in question its
merit, but a power of quite another kind, a power of
moral and spiritual emotion. But the power of
Greek radiance Goethe could give to his handling of
nature, and nobly too, as any one who will read his
*Wanderer*²—the poem in which a wanderer falls in
with a peasant woman and her child by their hut.
built out of the ruins of a temple near Cuma—may
see. Only the power of natural magic Goethe does
not, I think, give ; whereas Keats passes at will from
the Greek power to that power which is, as I say,
Celtic ; from his

"What little town, by river or seashore,"

to his

"White hawthorn and the pastoral eglantine,
Fast-fading violets cover'd up in leaves,"—

or his

. . . "magic casements, opening on the foam
Of perilous seas, in fairy lands forlorn,"—

---

¹ [" Der Morgen kam ; es scheuchten seine Tritte."]
² [" Gott segne dich, junge Frau."]

in which the very same note is struck as in those extracts which I quoted from Celtic romance, and struck with authentic and unmistakable power.

Shakespeare, in handling nature, touches this Celtic note so exquisitely, that perhaps one is inclined to be always looking for the Celtic note in him, and not to recognize his Greek note when it comes. But if one attends well to the difference between the two notes, and bears in mind, to guide one, such things as Virgil's " moss-grown springs and grass softer than sleep,"

> " Muscosi fontes et somno mollior herba;"

as his charming flower-gatherer, who

> " Pallentes violas et summa papavera carpens
> Narcissum et florem jungit bene olentis anethi;"

as his quinces and chestnuts,

> . . . '' cana legam tenera lanugine mala
> Castaneasque nuces,". . . . .

—then, I think, we shall be disposed to say that in Shakespeare's

> '' I know a bank where the wild thyme blows,
> Where oxlips and the nodding violet grows,
> Quite over-canopied with luscious woodbine,
> With sweet musk-roses and with eglantine,"

it is mainly a Greek note which is struck. Then, again in his

> . . . . . " look how the floor of heaven
> Is thick inlaid with patines of bright gold !"

we are at the very point of transition from the Greek note to the Celtic; there is the Greek clearness and brightness, with the Celtic aërialness and magic coming in.   Then we have the sheer, inimitable Celtic note in passages like this

> "Met we on hill, in dale, forest or mead,
>   By paved fountain or by rushy brook,
>   Or in the beached margent of the sea;"

or this, the last I will quote :

> "The moon shines bright.   In such a night as this,
>   When the sweet wind did gently kiss the trees,
>   And they did make no noise, in such a night
>   Troilus, methinks, mounted the Trojan walls—
>
> . . . . . . "in such a night
>   Did Thisbe fearfully o'ertrip the dew—
>
> . . . . . . "in such a night
>   *Stood Dido, with a willow in her hand*
>   *Upon the wild sea-banks, and waved her love*
>   *To come again to Carthage.*"

And those last lines of all are so drenched and intoxicated with the fairy-dew of that natural magic which is our theme, that I cannot do better than end with them.

From Translating Homer.

——The eccentricity, too, the arbitrariness, of which Mr. Newman's conception of Homer offers so signal an example, are not a peculiar failing of Mr. Newman's own ; in varying degrees they are the great defect of English intellect, the great blemish of English literature.   Our literature of the eighteenth century, the literature of the school of Dryden, Addison, Pope, Johnson, is a long reaction against this eccentricity, this arbitrariness; that reaction perished by its own faults, and its enemies are left once more masters of the field. It is much more likely that any new English version of Homer will have Mr. Newman's fault than Pope's. Our present literature, which is very far, certainly, from having the spirit and power of Elizabethan genius, yet has in its own way these faults, eccentricity and arbitrariness, quite as much as the Elizabethan literature ever had. They are the cause that, while upon none, perhaps, of the modern literatures has so great a sum of force been expended as upon the English literature, at the present hour this literature, regarded not as an object of mere literary interest but as a living intellectual instrument, ranks only third in European effect and importance among the literatures of Europe; it ranks after the literatures of France and Germany. Of these two literatures, as of the intellect of Europe in general, the main effort, for now many years, has been a *critical* effort; the endeavor, in all branches of knowledge, theology, philosophy, history, art, science,—to see the object as in itself it really is. But, owing to the presence in English literature of this eccentric and arbitrary spirit, owing to the strong tendency of English writers to bring to the consideration of their object some individual fancy, almost the last thing for which one would come to English literature is just that very thing which now Europe most desires—*criticism.* It is useful to notice any signal manifestation of those faults, which thus limit and

impair the action of our literature. And therefore
I have pointed out how widely, in translating Homer,
a man even of real ability and learning may go
astray, unless he brings to the study of this clearest
of poets one quality in which our English authors,
with all their great gifts, are apt to be somewhat
wanting—simple lucidity of mind.

—I said that Homer did not rise and sink with his
subject, was never to be called prosaic and low.
This gives surprise to many persons, who object that
parts of the *Iliad* are certainly pitched lower than
others, and who remind me of a number of absolutely level passages in Homer. But I never denied
that a *subject* must rise and sink, that it must have
its elevated and its level regions; all I deny is, that
a poet can be said to rise and sink when all that he,
as a poet, can do, is perfectly well done; when he is
perfectly sound and good, that is, perfect as a poet,
in the level regions of his subject as well as in its
elevated regions. Indeed, what distinguishes the
greatest masters of poetry from all others is, that
they are perfectly sound and poetical in these level
regions of their subject,—in these regions which are
the great difficulty of all poets but the very greatest,
which they never quite know what to do with. A
poet may sink in these regions by being falsely grand
as well as by being low; he sinks, in short, whenever
he does not treat his matter, whatever it is, in a
perfectly good and poetic way. But, so long as he
treats it in this way, he cannot be said to *sink*, what-

ever his matter may do. A passage of the simplest
narrative is quoted to me from Homer:

ὦτρυνεν δὲ ἕκαστον ἐποιχόμενος ἐπέεσσιν,
Μέσθλην τε, Γλαῦκόν τε, Μέδυντά τε, Θερσίλοχον τε ...

and I am asked whether Homer does not sink *there ;*
whether he " *can* have intended such lines as those
for poetry ?" My answer is : Those lines are very
good poetry indeed, poetry of the best class, *in that*
place. But when Wordsworth, having to narrate a
very plain matter, tries *not* to sink in narrating it,
tries, in short, to be what is falsely called poetical,
he does sink, although he sinks by being pompous,
not by being low.

> "Onward we drove beneath the Castle ; caught,
>   While crossing Magdalen Bridge, a glimpse of Cam,
>   And at the Hoop alighted, famous inn."

That last line shows excellently how a poet may
sink with his subject by resolving not to sink with
it. A page or two farther on, the subject rises to
grandeur, and then Wordsworth is nobly worthy of
it :

> " The antechapel, where the statue stood
>   Of Newton with his prism and silent face,
>   The marble index of a mind forever
>   Voyaging through strange seas of thought, alone."

But the supreme poet is he who is thoroughly sound
and poetical, alike when his subject is grand, and
when it is plain : with him the subject may sink, but
never the poet. But a Dutch painter does not rise
and sink with his subject,—Defoe, in *Moll Flanders,*
does not rise and sink with his subject,—in so far as

an artist cannot be said to sink who is sound in his
treatment of his subject, however plain it is : yet
Defoe, yet a Dutch painter, may in one sense be said
to sink with their subject, because though sound in
their treatment of it, they are not *poetical,*—poetical
in the true, not the false sense of the word ; because,
in fact, they are not in the grand style.   Homer can
in no sense be said to sink with his subject, because
his soundness has something more than literal natu-
ralness about it ; because his soundness is the soundness of Homer, of a great epic poet ; because, in
fact, he is in the grand style.   So he sheds over the
simplest matter he touches the charm of his grand
manner ; he makes everything noble.   Nothing has
raised more questioning among my critics than these
words,—*noble, the grand style.*   People complain
that I do not define these words sufficiently, that I
do not tell them enough about them.   " The grand .
style,—but what *is* the grand style ?"—they cry ;
some with an inclination to believe in it, but puzzled ;
others mockingly and with incredulity.   Alas! the
grand style is the last matter in the world for verbal
definition to deal with adequately.   One may say of
it as is said of faith : "One must feel it in order to
know what it is."   But, as of faith, so too one may
say of nobleness, of the grand style : "Woe to those
who know it not !"   Yet this expression, though in-
definable, has a charm ; one is the better for considering it ; *bonum est, nos hic esse ;* nay, one loves to
try to explain it, though one knows that one must
speak imperfectly.   For those, then, who ask the

question,—What is the grand style?—with sincerity,
I will try to make some answer, inadequate as it
must be.   For those who ask it mockingly I have
no answer, except to repeat to them, with compas-
sionate sorrow, the Gospel words: *Moriemini in
peccatis vestris,*—Ye shall die in your sins.

But let me, at any rate, have the pleasure of again
giving, before I begin to try and define the grand
style, a specimen of what it *is*.

> " Standing on earth, not rapt above the pole,
>   More safe I sing with mortal voice, unchanged
>   To hoarse or mute, though fall'n on evil days,
>   On evil days though fall'n, and evil tongues."....

There is the grand style in perfection ; and any one
who has a sense for it will feel it a thousand times
better from repeating those lines than from hearing
anything I can say about it.

Let us try, however, what *can* be said, controlling
what we say by examples.   I think it will be found
that the grand style arises in poetry, *when a noble
nature, poetically gifted, treats with simplicity or with
severity a serious subject*.   I think this definition will
be found to cover all instances of the grand style
in poetry which present themselves.   I think it will
be found to exclude all poetry which is not in
the grand style.   And I think it contains no terms
which are obscure, which themselves need defining.
Even those who do not understand what is meant
by calling poetry noble, will understand, I imagine,
what is meant by speaking of a noble nature in a
man.   But the noble or powerful nature—the *bedeu-*

tendes individuum of Goethe—is not enough. For instance, Mr. Newman has zeal for learning, zeal for thinking, zeal for liberty, and all these things are noble, they ennoble a man; but he has not the poetical gift: there must be the poetical gift, the "divine faculty," also. And, besides all this, the subject must be a serious one (for it is only by a kind of license that we can speak of the grand style in comedy); and it must be treated *with simplicity or severity.* Here is the great difficulty: the poets of the world have been many; there has been wanting neither abundance of poetical gift nor abundance of noble natures; but a poetical gift so happy, in a noble nature so circumstanced and trained, that the result is a continuous style, perfect in simplicity or perfect in severity, has been extremely rare. One poet has had the gifts of nature and faculty in unequalled fulness, without the circumstances and training which make this sustained perfection of style possible. Of other poets, some have caught this perfect strain now and then, in short pieces or single lines, but have not been able to maintain it through considerable works; others have composed all their productions in a style which, by comparison with the best, one must call secondary.

The best model of the grand style simple is Homer; perhaps the best model of the grand style severe is Milton. But Dante is remarkable for affording admirable examples of both styles; he has the grand style which arises from simplicity, and he has the grand style which arises from severity; and from

him I will illustrate them both.   In a former lecture
I pointed out what that severity of poetical style is,
which comes from saying a thing with a kind of intense compression, or in an allusive, brief, almost
haughty way, as if the poet's mind were charged
with so many and such grave matters, that he would
not deign to treat any one of them explicitly.   Of
this severity the last line of the following stanza of
the *Purgatory* is a good example.   Dante has been
telling Forese that Virgil had guided him though
Hell, and he goes on :

> " Indi m' han tratto su gli suoi conforti,
>   Salendo e rigirando la Montagna
>   *Che drizza voi che il mondo fece torti.*"

" Thence hath his comforting aid led me up, climb-
ing and circling the Mountain, *which straightens you
whom the world made crooked.*"   These last words,
" la Montagna *che drizza voi che il mondo fece torti,*"
—the Mountain *which straightens you whom the
world made crooked,*"—for the Mountain of Purgatory, I call an excellent specimen of the grand style
in severity, where the poet's mind is too full charged
to suffer him to speak more explicitly.   But the
very next stanza is a beautiful specimen of the grand
style in simplicity, where a noble nature and a poetical gift unite to utter a thing with the most limpid
plainness and clearness :

> " Tanto dice di farmi sua compagna
>   Ch' io sarò là dove fia Beatrice ;
>   Quivi convien che senza lui rimagna."

"So long," Dante continues, "so long he (Virgil) saith he will bear me company, until I shall be there where Beatrice is ; there it behoves that without him I remain." But the noble simplicity of that in the Italian no words of mine can render.

Both these styles, the simple and the severe, are truly grand ; the severe seems, perhaps, the grandest, so long as we attend most to the great personality, to the noble nature, in the poet its author ; the simple seems the grandest when we attend most to the exquisite faculty, to the poetical gift. But the simple is no doubt to be preferred. It is the more *magical :* in the other there is something intellectual, something which gives scope for a play of thought which may exist where the poetical gift is either wanting or present in only inferior degree : the severe is much more imitable, and this a little spoils its charm. A kind of semblance of this style keeps Young going, one may say, through all the nine parts of that most indifferent production, the *Night Thoughts.* But the grand style in simplicity is inimitable.

——When Mr. Spedding talks of a plainness of thought *like Homer's,* of a plainness of speech *like Homer's,* and says that he finds these constantly in Mr. Tennyson's poetry, I answer that these I do not find there at all. Mr. Tennyson is a most distinguished and charming poet ; but the very essential characteristic of his poetry is, it seems to me, an extreme subtlety and curious elaborateness of thought, an extreme subtlety and curious elaborate-

ness of expression. In the best and most characteristic productions of his genius, these characteristics
are most prominent. They are marked characteristics, as we have seen, of the Elizabethan poets;
they are marked, though not the essential, characteristics of Shakespeare himself. Under the influences of the nineteenth century, under wholly new
conditions of thought and culture, they manifest
themselves in Mr. Tennyson's poetry in a wholly
new way. But they are still there. The essential
bent of his poetry is towards such expressions as—

> " Now lies the Earth all Danaë to the stars ;"
>
> > " O'er the sun's bright eye
> > Drew the vast eyelid of an inky cloud ;"
>
> " When the cairned mountain was a shadow, sunned
> The world to peace again ;"
>
> " The fresh young captains flashed their glittering teeth,
> The huge bush-bearded barons heaved and blew ;"
>
> " He bared the knotted column of his throat,
> The massive square of his heroic breast,
> And arms on which the standing muscle sloped
> As slopes a wild brook o'er a little stone,
> Running too vehemently to break upon it."

And this way of speaking is the least *plain*, the
most *un-Homeric*, which can possibly be conceived.
Homer presents his thought to you just as it wells
from the source of his mind: Mr. Tennyson carefully distils his thought before he will part with it.
Hence comes, in the expression of the thought, a
heightened and elaborate air. In Homer's poetry
it is all natural thoughts in natural words; in Mr.

Tennyson's poetry it is all distilled thoughts in distilled words. Exactly this heightening and elabora-
tion may be observed in Mr. Spedding's

" While the steeds *mouthed their corn aloof* "

(an expression which might have been Mr. Tennyson's), on which I have already commented; and to
one who is penetrated with a sense of the real simplicity of Homer, this subtle sophistication of the
thought is, I think, very perceptible even in such
lines as these,—

" And drunk delight of battle with my peers,
Far on the ringing plains of windy Troy,"—

which I have seen quoted as perfectly Homeric.
Perfect simplicity can be obtained only by a genius
of which perfect simplicity is an essential characteristic.

So true is this, that when a genius essentially
subtle, or a genius which, from whatever cause, is in
its essence not truly and broadly simple, determines
to be perfectly plain, determines not to admit a
shade of subtlety or curiosity into its expression, it
cannot ever then attain real simplicity; it can only
attain a semblance of simplicity.[1] French criticism,
richer in its vocabulary than ours, has invented a
useful word to distinguish this semblance (often

---

[1] I speak of poetic genius as employing itself upon narrative or
dramatic poetry,—poetry in which the poet has to go out of himself
and to create. In lyrical poetry, in the direct expression of personal feeling, the most subtle genius may, under the momentary
pressure of passion, express itself simply. Even here, however,
the native tendency will generally be discernible.

very beautiful and valuable) from the real quality.
The real quality it calls *simplicité*, the semblance
simplesse. The one is natural simplicity, the other
is artificial simplicity. What is called simplicity in
the productions of a genius essentially not simple,
is, in truth, *simplesse*. The two are distinguishable
from one another the moment they appear in company. For instance, let us take the opening of the
narrative in Wordsworth's *Michael :*

> " Upon the forest-side in Grasmere Vale
>   There dwelt a shepherd, Michael was his name ;
>   An old man, stout of heart, and strong of limb.
>   His bodily frame had been from youth to age
>   Of an unusual strength ; his mind was keen, ˙
>   Intense, and frugal, apt for all affairs ;
>   And in his shepherd's calling he was prompt
>   And watchful more than ordinary men."

Now let us take the opening of the narrative in Mr.
Tennyson's *Dora :*

> " With Farmer Allan at the farm abode
>   William and Dora. William was his son,
>   And she his niece. He often looked at them,
>   And often thought, ' I'll make them man and wife.' "

The simplicity of the first of these passages is *simplicité ;* that of the second, *simplesse*. Let us take the
end of the same two poems : first, of *Michael :*

> " The cottage which was named the Evening Star
>   Is gone,—the ploughshare has been through the ground
>   On which it stood ; great changes have been wrought
>   In all the neighborhood : yet the oak is left
>   That grew beside their door : and the remains
>   Of the unfinished sheepfold may be seen
>   Beside the boisterous brook of Green-head Ghyll."

And now, of *Dora :*

> " So those four abode
> Within one house together; and as years
> Went forward, Mary took another mate :
> But Dora lived unmarried till her death."

A heedless critic may call both of these passages simple if he will. Simple, in a certain sense, they both are ; but between the simplicity of the two there is all the difference that there is between the simplicity of Homer and the simplicity of Moschus. ——When there comes in poetry what I may call the *lyrical cry,* this transfigures everything, makes everything grand ; the simplest form may be here even an advantage, because the flame of the emotion glows through and through it more easily. To go again for an illustration to Wordsworth ;—our great poet, since Milton, by his performance, as Keats, I think, is our great poet by his gift and promise ;—in one of his stanzas to the Cuckoo, we have :—

> " And I can listen to thee yet ;
> Can lie upon the plain
> And listen, till I do beget
> That golden time again."

Here the lyrical cry, though taking the simple balladform, is as grand as the lyrical cry coming in poetry of an ampler form.

From the Essay on the Function of Criticism at the Present Time.

The critical power is of lower rank than the creative. True ; but in assenting to this proposition

one or two things are to be kept in mind. It is
undeniable that the exercise of a creative power,
that a free creative activity, is the highest function
of man; it is proved to be so by man's finding in it
his true happiness. But it is undeniable, also, that
men may have the sense of exercising this free
creative activity in other ways than in producing
great works of literature or art; if it were not so,
all but a very few men would be shut out from the
true happiness of all men. They may have it in
well-doing, they may have it in learning, they may
have it even in criticising. This is one thing to be
kept in mind. Another is, that the exercise of the
creative power in the production of great works of
literature or art, however high this exercise of it
may rank, is not at all epochs and under all conditions possible; and that therefore labor may be
vainly spent in attempting it, which might with
more fruit be used in preparing for it, in rendering
it possible. This creative power works with elements, with materials; what if it has not those
materials, those elements, ready for its use? In
that case it must surely wait till they are ready.
Now, in literature—I will limit myself to literature,
for it is about literature that the question arises—
the elements with which the creative power works
are ideas; the best ideas on every matter which
literature touches, current at the time. At any rate
we may lay it down as certain that in modern literature no manifestation of the creative power not
working with these can be very important or fruitful.

And I say *current* at the time, not merely accessible at the time; for creative literary genius does not principally show itself in discovering new ideas: that is rather the business of the philosopher. The grand work of literary genius is a work of synthesis and exposition, not of analysis and discovery; its gift lies in the faculty of being happily inspired by a certain intellectual and spiritual atmosphere, by a certain order of ideas, when it finds itself in them; of dealing divinely with these ideas, presenting them in the most effective and attractive combinations, —making beautiful works with them, in short. But it must have the atmosphere, it must find itself amidst the order of ideas, in order to work freely; and these it is not so easy to command. This is why great creative epochs in literature are so rare, this is why there is so much that is unsatisfactory in the productions of many men of real genius; because, for the creation of a master-work of literature two powers must concur,—the power of the man and the power of the moment, and the man is not enough without the moment; the creative power has, for its happy exercise, appointed elements, and those elements are not in its own control.

Nay, they are more within the control of the critical power. It is the business of the critical power, as I said in the words already quoted, "in all branches of knowledge, theology, philosophy, history, art, science, to see the object as in itself it really is." Thus it tends at last to make an intellectual situation of which the creative power can

profitably avail itself. It tends to establish an order
of ideas, if not absolutely true, yet true by comparison with that which it displaces ; to make the best
ideas prevail. Presently these new ideas reach society, the touch of truth is the touch of life, and
there is a stir and growth everywhere ; out of this
stir and growth come the creative epochs of literature.

Or, to narrow our range, and quit these considerations of the general march of genius and of society,
—considerations which are apt to become too abstract and impalpable,—every one can see that a
poet, for instance, ought to know life and the world
before dealing with them in poetry; and life and
the world being in modern times very complex
things, the creation of a modern poet, to be worth
much, implies a great critical effort behind it ; else
it must be a comparatively poor, barren, and short-
lived affair. This is why Byron's poetry had so
little endurance in it, and Goethe's so much: both
Byron and Goethe had a great productive power,
but Goethe's was nourished by a great critical effort
providing the true materials for it, and Byron's was
not ; Goethe knew life and the world, the poet's
necessary subjects, much more comprehensively and
thoroughly than Byron. He knew a great deal more
of them, and he knew them much more as they
really are.

It has long seemed to me that the burst of creative activity in our literature, through the first
quarter of this century, had about it in fact some-

thing premature; and that from this cause its productions are doomed, most of them, in spite of the
sanguine hopes which accompanied and do still
accompany them, to prove hardly more lasting than
the productions of far less splendid epochs. And
this prematureness comes from its having proceeded
without having its proper data, without sufficient
materials to work with. In other words, the English
poetry of the first quarter of this century, with
plenty of creative force, plenty of energy, did not
know enough. This makes Byron so empty of
matter, Shelley so incoherent, Wordsworth even,
profound as he is, yet so wanting in completeness
and variety. Wordsworth cared little for books,
and disparaged Goethe. But surely the one thing
wanting to make Wordsworth an even greater poet
than he is,—his thought richer, and his influence
of wider application,—was that he should have read
more books, among them, no doubt, those of that
Goethe whom he disparaged without reading him.

But to speak of books and reading may easily
lead to a misunderstanding here. It was not really
books and reading that lacked to our poetry at this
epoch; Shelley had plenty of reading, Coleridge
had immense reading. Pindar and Sophocles—as
we all say so glibly, and often with so little discern-
ment of the real import of what we are saying—had
not many books; Shakespeare was no deep reader.
True; but in the Greece of Pindar and Sophocles,
in the England of Shakespeare, the poet lived in a
current of ideas in the highest degree animating

and nourishing to the creative power; society was, in the fullest measure, permeated by fresh thought, intelligent and alive. And this state of things is the true basis for the creative power's exercise: in this it finds its data, its materials, truly ready for its hand; all the books and reading in the world are only valuable as they are helps to this. Even when this does not actually exist, books and reading may enable a man to construct a kind of semblance of it in his own mind, a world of knowledge and intelligence in which he may live and work. This is by no means an equivalent to the artist for the nationally diffused life and thought of the epochs of Sophocles or Shakespeare; but, besides that it may be a means of preparation for such epochs, it does really constitute, if many share in it, a quickening and sustaining atmosphere of great value. Such an atmosphere the many-sided learning and the long and widely combined critical effort of Germany formed for Goethe when he lived and worked. There was no national glow of life and thought there as in the Athens of Pericles or the England of Elizabeth. That was the poet's weakness. But there was a sort of equivalent for it in the complete culture and unfettered thinking of a large body of Germans. That was his strength. In the England of the first quarter of this century there was neither a national glow of life and thought, such as we had in the age of Elizabeth, nor yet a culture and a force of learning and criticism such as were to be found in Germany. Therefore the creative power of poetry wanted, for success in the highest sense, materials, and a basis; a thorough interpretation of the world was necessarily denied to it.

But then comes another question as to the sub-ject-matter which literary criticism should most seek. Here, in general, its course is determined for it by the idea which is the law of its being; the idea of a disinterested endeavor to learn and propagate the best that is known and thought in the world, and thus to establish a current of fresh and true ideas. By the very nature of things, as England is not all the world, much of the best that is known and thought in the world cannot be of English growth, must be foreign; by the nature of things, again, it is just this that we are least likely to know, while English thought is streaming in upon us from all sides, and takes excellent care that we shall not be ignorant of its existence. The English critic of literature, therefore, must dwell much on foreign thought, and with particular heed on any part of it, which, while significant and fruitful in itself, is for any reason specially likely to escape him. Again, judging is often spoken of as the critic's one business, and so in some sense it is; but the judgment which almost insensibly forms itself in a fair and clear mind, along with fresh knowledge, is the valuable one; and thus knowledge, and ever fresh knowledge, must be the critic's great concern for himself. And it is by communicating fresh knowledge, and letting his own judgment pass along with it,—but insensibly, and in the second place, not the first, as a sort of companion and clue, not as an abstract lawgiver,—that the critic will generally do most good to his readers.

" In France," says M. Saint-Beuve, " the first consideration for us is not whether we are amused and pleased by a work of art or mind, nor is it whether we are touched by it. What we seek above all to learn is, whether *we were right* in being amused with it, and in applauding it, and in being moved by it."

Those are very remarkable words, and they are, I believe, in the main quite true. A Frenchman has, to a considerable degree, what one may call a conscience in intellectual matters; he has an active belief that there is a right and a wrong in them, that he is bound to honor and obey the right, that he is disgraced by cleaving to the wrong. All the world has, or professes to have, this conscience in moral matters. The word *conscience* has become almost confined, in popular use, to the moral sphere, because this lively susceptibility of feeling is, in the moral sphere, so far more common than in the intellectual sphere; the livelier, in the moral sphere, this susceptibility is, the greater becomes a man's readiness to admit a high standard of action, an ideal authoritatively correcting his everyday moral habits; here, such willing admission of authority is due to sensitiveness of conscience. And a like deference to a standard higher than one's own habitual standard in intellectual matters, a like respectful recognition of a superior ideal is caused, in the intellectual sphere, by sensitiveness of intelligence.

From the Essay on the Literary Influence of Academies.

In a production which we have all been reading lately, a production stamped throughout with a literary quality very rare in this country, and of which I shall have a word to say presently—*urbanity ;* in this production, the work of a man never to be named by any son of Oxford without sympathy, a man who alone in Oxford of his generation, alone of many generations, conveyed to us in his genius that same charm, that same ineffable sentiment which this exquisite place itself conveys,—I mean Dr. Newman,—an expression is frequently used which is more common in theological than in literary language, but which seems to me fitted to be of general service,—the *note* of so and so, the note of catholicity, the note of antiquity, the note of sanctity, and so on. Adopting this expressive word, I say that in the bulk of the intellectual work of a nation which has no centre, no intellectual metropolis like an academy, like M. Sainte-Beuve's "sovereign organ of opinion," like M. Renan's " recognized authority in matters of tone and taste," there is observable a *note of provinciality.* Now to get rid of provinciality is a certain stage of culture ; a stage the positive result of which we must not make of too much importance, but which is, nevertheless, indispensable, for it brings us on to the platform where alone the best and highest intellectual work can be said fairly to begin. Work done after men have reached this platform is *classical;* and that is the only work which, in the long-run, can stand. All the *scoriæ* in the work of men of great genius who have not lived on this platform are due to their not having lived on it. Genius raises them to it by moments, and the portions of their work which are immortal are done at these moments; but more of it would have been immortal if they had not reached this platform at moments only, if they had had the culture which makes men live there.

The less a literature has felt the influence of a supposed centre of correct information, correct judgment, correct taste, the more we shall find in it this note of provinciality. I have shown the note of provinciality as caused by remoteness from a centre of correct information. Of course the note of provinciality from the want of a centre of correct taste is still more visible, and it is also still more common. For here great—even the greatest—powers of mind must fail a man. Great powers of mind will make him inform himself thoroughly, great powers of mind will make him think profoundly, even with ignorance and platitude all round him; but not even great powers of mind will keep his taste and style perfectly sound and sure, if he is left too much to himself, with no " sovereign organ of opinion " in these matters near him. Even men like Jeremy Taylor and Burke suffer here. Take this passage from Taylor's funeral sermon on Lady Carbery; "So have I seen a river, deep and smooth, passing with a still foot and a sober face, and paying to the *fiscus*, the great exchequer of the sea, a tribute large and full; and hard by it a little brook, skipping and making a noise upon its unequal and neighbor bottom ; and after all its talking and bragged motion, it paid to its common audit no more than the revenues of a little cloud or a contemptible vessel: so have I sometimes compared the issues of her religion to the solemnities and famed outsides of another's piety."

That passage has been much admired, and, indeed, the genius in it is undeniable. I should say, for my part, that genius, the ruling divinity of poetry, had been too busy in it, and intelligence, the ruling divinity of prose, not busy enough. But can any one, with the best models of style in his head, help feeling the note of provinciality there, the want of simplicity, the want of measure, the want of just the qualities that make prose classical ? If he does not feel what I mean, let him place beside the passage of Taylor this passage from the Panegyric of St. Paul, by Taylor's contemporary, Bossuet :

"Il ira, cet ignorant dans l'art de bien dire, avec cette locution rude, avec cette phrase qui sent l'étranger, il ira en cette Grèce polie, la mère des philosophes et des orateurs ; et malgré la résistance du monde, il y établira plus d'Eglises que Platon n'y a gagné de disciples par cette éloquence qu'on a crue divine."

There we have prose without the note of provinciality—classical prose, prose of the centre.

Or take Burke, our greatest English prose-writer,
as I think ; take expressions like this :

" I confess I never liked this continual talk of
resistance and revolution, or the practice of making
the extreme medicine of the constitution its daily
bread.   It renders the habit of society dangerously
valetudinary ; it is taking periodical doses of mercury
sublimate, and swallowing down repeated provoca-
tions of cantharides to our love of liberty. . . ."

I say that is extravagant prose ; prose too much
suffered to indulge its caprices ; prose at too great a
distance from the centre of good taste ; prose, in
short, with the note of provinciality.   People may
reply, it is rich and imaginative ; yes, that is just it,
it is *Asiatic* prose, as the ancient critics would have
said ; prose somewhat barbarously rich and over-
loaded.   But the true prose is Attic prose.

Well, but Addison's prose is Attic prose.   Where,
then, it may be asked, is the note of provinciality in
Addison ?   I answer, in the commonplace of his
ideas.   This is a matter worth remarking.   Addison
claims to take leading rank as a moralist.   To do
that, you must have ideas of the first order on your
subject—the best ideas, at any rate, attainable in
your time—as well as be able to express them in a
perfectly sound and sure style.   Else you show your
distance from the centre of ideas by your matter ;
you are provincial by your matter, though you may
not be provincial by your style.   It is comparatively

a small matter to express oneself well, if one will be
content with not expressing much, with expressing
only trite ideas; the problem is to express new and
profound ideas in a perfectly sound and classical
style. He is the true classic, in every age, who does
that. Now Addison has not, on his subject of
morals, the force of ideas of the moralists of the first
class—the classical moralists; he has not the best
ideas attainable in or about his time, and which were,
so to speak, in the air then, to be seized by the finest
spirits; he is not be compared for power, searching-
ness, or delicacy of thought to Pascal or La Bruyère or Vauvenargues; he is rather on a level, in this
respect, with a man like Marmontel. Therefore, I
say, he has the note of provinciality as a moralist;
he is provincial by his matter, though not by his
style.

To illustrate what I mean by an example. Addison, writing as a moralist on fixedness in religious
faith, says :

"Those who delight in reading books of controversy do very seldom arrive at a fixed and settled
habit of faith. The doubt which was laid revives
again, and shows itself in new difficulties; and that
generally for this reason,—because the mind, which
is perpetually tossed in controversies and disputes,
is apt to forget the reasons which had once set it to
rest, and to be disquieted with any former perplexity
when it appears in a new shape, or is started by a
different hand."

It may be said, that is classical English, perfect in

lucidity, measure, and propriety. I make no objection; but, in my turn, I say that the idea expressed is perfectly trite and barren, and that it is a note of provinciality in Addison, in a man whom a nation puts forward as one of its great moralists, to have no profounder and more striking idea to produce on this great subject. Compare, on the same subject, these words of a moralist really of the first order, really at the centre by his ideas,—Joubert :—

"L'expérience de beaucoup d'opinions donne a l'esprit beaucoup de flexibilité et l'affermit dans celles qu'il croit les meieleures."

With what a flash of light that touches the subject! how it sets us thinking! what a genuine contribution to moral science it is!

In short, where there is no centre like an academy, if you have genius and powerful ideas, you are apt not to have the best style going; if you have precision of style and not genius, you are apt not to have the best ideas going.

The provincial spirit, again, exaggerates the value of its ideas for want of a high standard at hand by which to try them. Or rather, for want of such a standard, it gives one idea too much prominence at the expense of others; it orders its ideas amiss; it is hurried away by fancies; it likes and dislikes too passionately, too exclusively. Its admiration weeps hysterical tears, and its disapprobation foams at the mouth. So we get the *eruptive* and the *aggressive* manner in literature; the former prevails most in our criticism, the latter in our newspapers. For, not having the lucidity of a large and centrally placed intelligence, the provincial spirit has not its gracious-ness; it does not persuade, it makes war; it has not urbanity, the tone of the city, of the centre, the tone which always aims at a spiritual and intellectual effect, and not excluding the use of banter, never disjoins banter itself from politeness, from felicity.

From the Essay on Maurice Guerin.

The grand power of poetry is in its interpretative power; by which I mean, not a power of drawing out in black and white an explanation of the mys-tery of the universe, but the power of so dealing with things as to awaken in us a wonderfully full, new, and intimate sense of them, and of our relations with them. When this sense is awakened in us, as to objects without us, we feel ourselves to be in contact with the essential nature of these objects, to be no longer bewildered and oppressed by them, but to have their secret, and to be in harmony with them ; and this feeling calms and satisfies us as no other can. Poetry, indeed, interprets in another way be-sides this; but one of its two ways of interpreting, of exercising its highest power, is by awakening this sense in us. I will not now inquire whether this sense is illusive, whether it does absolutely make us possess the real nature of things; all I can say is, that poetry can awaken it in us, and that to awaken it in us is one of the highest powers of poe-try. The interpretations of science do not give us this intimate sense of objects as the interpretations of poetry give it ; they appeal to a limited faculty, and not to the whole man. It is not Linnæus or Cavendish or Cuvier who gives us the true sense of animals, or water, or plants, who seizes their secret for us, who makes us participate in their life ; it is Shakespeare, with his

> " Daffodils
> That come before the swallow dares, and take
> The winds of March with beauty ;"

it is Wordsworth, with his

> " Voice . . . . heard
> In spring-time from the cuckoo-bird,
> Breaking the silence of the seas
> Among the farthest Hebrides ;"

it is Keats, with his

> " moving waters at their priestlike task
> Of cold ablution round Earth's human shores ;"

it is Chateaubriand, with his, " *cîme indéterminée des forêts ;*" it is Senancour, with his mountain birch-tree : " *cette écorce blanche, lisse et crevassée ; cette tige agreste ; ces branches qui s'inclinent vers la terre ; la mobilité des feuilles, et tout cet abandon, simplicité de la nature, attitude des déserts.*"

JAMES RUSSELL LOWELL.

1819–1891.

[Mr. Lowell's literary essays represent the highest order of criticism that has appeared in America. The two volumes of " Among My Books " and the collection called " My Study Windows " contain strong and original thought, unusual scholarship, and a poet's own power of feeling for poetry. Mr. Lowell was learned, and his learning did not dull him æsthetically, or blur his tact in distinguishing relative literary values. In criticism, as in his whole broad nature, he grew better as he grew old. Though the latter part of his life was not concentrated upon literature, his last essays are even superior in manner to the more elaborate works of his prime, and if less copiously instructive, are still more agreeable. The concluding pages of one of these, the essay on Gray, are given here, by permission of Messrs. Houghton, Miflin & Co.]

From the Essay on Gray, in "Last Essays."

IN spite of unjust depreciation and misapplied criticism, Gray holds his own and bids fair to last as long as the language which he knew how to write so well and of which he is one of the glories. Wordsworth is justified in saying that he helped himself from everybody and everywhere ; and yet he made such admirable use of what he stole (if theft there was) that we should as soon think of finding fault with a man for pillaging the dictionary. He mixed himself with whatever he took—an incalculable increment.   In the editions of his poems, the thin line of text stands at the top of the page like cream, and below it is the skim-milk drawn from many milky mothers of the herd out of which it is risen.   But the thing to be considered is that, no matter where the material came from, the result is Gray's own.   Whether original or not, he knew how to make a poem,—a vary rare knowledge among men.   The thought in Gray is neither uncommon nor profound, and you may call it beatified commonplace if you choose.   I shall not contradict you.   I have lived long enough to know that there is a vast deal of commonplace in the world of no particular use to anybody, and am thankful to the man who has the divine gift to idealize it for me.   Nor am I offended with the odor of the library that hangs about Gray, for it recalls none but delightful sensations.   It was in the very best literature that Gray was steeped, and I am glad that both he and we should profit by it.   If he appropriated a fine phrase wherever he found it, it was by right of eminent domain, for surely he was one of the masters of language.   His praise is that what he touched was idealized, and kindled with some virtue that was not there before, but came from him.

And he was the most conscientious of artists. Some of the verses which he discards in reference to this conscientiousness of form which sacrifices the poet to the poem, the part to the whole, and regards nothing but the effect to be produced, would have

made the fortune of another poet. Take, for example, this stanza omitted from the " Elegy" (just before
the epitaph), because, says Mason, " he thought it
was too long a parenthesis in this place :"

> " There scattered oft, the earliest of the year,
>   By hands unseen are showers of violets found ;
> The redbreast loves to build and warble there,
> And little footsteps lightly print the ground."

Gray might run his pen through this, but he could
not obliterate it from the memory of men. Surely
Wordsworth himself never achieved a simplicity of
language so pathetic in suggestion, so musical in
movement as this.

Any slave of the mine may find the rough gem,
but it is the cutting and polishing that reveal its
heart of fire ; it is the setting that makes of it a
jewel to hang at the ear of Time. If Gray cull his
words and phrases here, there, and everywhere, it is
he who charges them with the imagination or picturesque touch which only he could give and which
makes them magnetic. For example, in these two
verses of " The Bard :"

> " Amazement in his van with Flight combined,
> And Sorrow's faded form and Solitude behind !"

The suggestion (we are informed by the notes)
came from Cowper and Oldham, and the amaze-
ment *combined* with flight sticks fast in prose. But
the personification of Sorrow and the fine generaliza-
tion of Solitude in the last verse which gives an
imaginative reach to the whole passage are Gray's

own. The owners of what Gray "conveyed" would have found it hard to identify their property and prove title to it after it had once suffered the Gray-change by steeping in his mind and memory.

When the example in our Latin Grammar tells us that *Mors communis est omnibus*, it states a truism of considerable interest, indeed, to the person in whose particular case it is to be illustrated, but neither new nor startling. No one would think of citing it, whether to produce conviction or to heighten discourse. Yet mankind are agreed in finding something more poignant in the same reflection when Horace tells us that the palace as well as the hovel shudders at the indiscriminating foot of Death. Here is something more than the dry statement of a truism. The difference between the two is that between a lower and a higher; it is, in short, the difference between prose and poetry. The oyster has begun, at least, to secrete its pearl, something identical with its shell in substance, but in sentiment and association how unlike! Malherbe takes the same image and makes it a little more picturesque, though, at the same time, I fear, a little more Parisian, too, when he says that the sentinel pacing before the gate of the Louvre cannot forbid Death an entrance to the King. And how long had not that comparison between the rose's life and that of the maiden dying untimely been a commonplace when the same Malherbe made it irreclaimably his own by mere felicity of phrase? We do not ask where people got their hints, but what they made

out of them. The commonplace is unhappily within
reach of us all, and unhappily, too, they are rare
who can give it novelty and even invest it with a
kind of grandeur as Gray knew how to do. If his
poetry be a mosaic, the design is always his own.
He, if any, had certainly "the last and greatest art,"
— the art to please. Shall we deny ourselves to the
charm of sentiment because we prefer the electric
shudder that imagination gives us? Even were
Gray's claims to being a great poet rejected, he can
never be classed with the many, so great and uniform are the efficacy of his phrase and the music to
which he sets it. This unique distinction, at least,
may be claimed for him without dispute, that he is
the one English poet who has written less and
pleased more than any other. Above all, it is as a
teacher of the art of writing that he is to be valued.
If there be any well of English undefiled, it is to be
found in him and his master, Dryden. They are
still standards of what may be called classical English, neither archaic nor modern, and as far removed
from pedantry as from vulgarity. They were

> " Tous deux disciples d'une escole
> Où l'on forcene doucement,"

·—a school in which have been enrolled the Great
Masters of literature.

JOHN RUSKIN.

1819

[Ruskin's literary criticism is to be found scattered all
through his writings, sometimes in the most unexpected
connections. On specific passages he is frequently unre
liable, inasmuch as he is at times carried away by his sensibility, or by that capricious quality of his genius that
renders him on almost all subjects a partially unbalanced
writer. Nothing, for instance, could be much more uncriti-
cal than the extent to which he pushes his interpretation of
the lines in *Lycidas*, on which he comments in a well-known
passage of *Sesame and Lilies*. In reading him it is necessary to decline to assume the attitude that he somewhere
recommends readers to take—that of the docile and acquies-
cent pupil. But in spite of his being occasionally fanciful
and erratic, his unusual poetic feeling, his deep sympathies,
and the force and beauty of his expression give to many of his
literary excursions great interest and value. Nor is he
without a high order of intellectual insight, as is shown in
the following discussion of what he calls the Pathetic
Fallacy; though even here, at one point, he gives a singular
illustration of the fault he is condemning. The selection is
from the third volume of *Modern Painters*. In the preceding paragraphs he has been objecting, in his usual attitude towards .metaphysics, to the use of the words "objec-
tive" and "subjective" in criticism.]

From Modern Painters, Vol. III, Chapter XII.

NOW, therefore, putting these tiresome and absurd
words quite out of our way, we may go on at our

case to examine the point in question, namely, the difference between the ordinary, proper, and true appearances of things to us; and the extraordinary, or false appearances, when we are under the influence of emotion, or contemplative fancy;[1] false appearances, I say, as being entirely unconnected with any real power or character in the object, and only imputed to it by us.

For instance—

> " The spendthrift crocus, bursting through the mould
> Naked and shivering, with his cup of gold."[2]

This is very beautiful, and yet very untrue. The crocus is not a spendthrift, but a hardy plant; its yellow is not gold, but saffron. How is it that we enjoy so much the having it put into our heads that it is anything else than a plain crocus?

It is an important question. For, throughout our past reasonings about art, we have always found that nothing could be good or useful, or ultimately pleasurable, which was untrue. But here is something pleasurable in written poetry which is nevertheless *un*true. And what is more, if we think over our favorite poetry, we shall find it full of this kind of fallacy, and that we like it all the more for being so.

It will appear also, on consideration of the matter, that this fallacy is of two principal kinds. Either,

---

[1] [" The contemplative fancy summons images of external relationship."]

[2] Holmes.

as in this case of the crocus, it is the fallacy of wilful fancy, which involves no real expectation that it will be believed; or else it is a fallacy caused by an excited state of the feelings, making us, for the time, more or less irrational. Of the cheating of the fancy we shall have to speak presently; but, in this chapter, I want to examine the nature of the other error, that which the mind admits, when affected strongly by emotion. Thus, for instance, in Alton Locke,—

> " They rowed her in across the rolling foam—
> The cruel, crawling foam."

The foam is not cruel, neither does it crawl. The state of mind which attributes to it these characters of a living creature is one in which the reason is unhinged by grief. All violent feelings have the same effect. They produce in us a falseness in all our impressions of external things, which I would generally characterize as the " Pathetic fallacy."

Now we are in the habit of considering this fallacy as eminently a character of poetical description, and the temper of mind in which we allow it, as one eminently poetical, because passionate. But I believe, if we look well into the matter, that we shall find the greatest poets do not often admit this kind of falseness,—that it is only the second order of poets who much delight in it.[1]

---

[1] I admit two orders of poets, but no third : and by these two orders I mean the Creative (Shakespeare, Homer, Dante), and Reflective or Perceptive (Wordsworth, Keats, Tennyson). But both of these must be *first*-rate in their range, though their range is different ; and with poetry second-rate in *quality* no·one ought

Thus, when Dante describes the spirits falling from the bank of Acheron "as dead leaves flutter from a bough," he gives the most perfect image possible of their utter lightness, feebleness, passiveness, and scattering agony of despair, without, however, for an instant losing his own clear perception that *these* are souls, and *those* are leaves: he makes no confusion of one with the other. But when Coleridge speaks of

> " The one red leaf. the last of its clan,
> That dances as often as dance it can,"

---

to be allowed to trouble mankind. There is quite enough of the best,—much more than we can ever read or enjoy in the length of a life; and it is a literal wrong or sin in any person to encumber us with inferior work. I have no patience with apologies made by young pseudo-poets, " that they believe there is *some* good in what they have written: that they hope to do better in time," etc. *Some* good ! If there is not *all* good, there is no good. If they ever hope to do better, why do they trouble us now ? Let them rather courageously burn all they have done, and wait for the better days. There are few men, ordinarily educated, who in moments of strong feeling could not strike out a poetical thought, and afterwards polish it so as to be presentable. But men of sense know better than so to waste their time ; and those who sincerely love poetry, know the touch of the master's hand on the chords too well to fumble among them after him. Nay, more than this : all inferior poetry is an injury to the good, inasmuch as it takes away the freshness of rhymes, blunders upon and gives a wretched commonalty to good thoughts ; and, in general, adds to the weight of human weariness in a most woful and culpable manner. There are few thoughts likely to come across ordinary men, which have not already been expressed by greater men in the best possible way; and it is a wiser, more generous, more noble thing to remember and point out the perfect words, than to invent poorer ones, wherewith to encumber temporarily the world.

he has a morbid, that is to say, a so far false, idea about the leaf : he fancies a life in it, and will, which there are not ; confuses its powerlessness with choice, its fading death with merriment, and the wind that shakes it with music.   Here, however, there is some beauty, even in the morbid passage ; but take an instance in Homer and Pope.   Without the knowledge of Ulysses, Elpenor, his youngest follower, has fallen from an upper chamber in the Circean palace, and has been left dead, unmissed by his leader, or companions, in the haste of their departure.   They cross the sea to the Cimmerian land ; and Ulysses summons the shades from Tartarus.   The first which appears is that of the lost Elpenor.   Ulysses, amazed, and in exactly the spirit of bitter and terrified lightness which is seen in Hamlet,[1] addresses the spirit with the simple, startled words :

"Elpenor?   How camest thou under the Shadowy darkness ?   Hast thou come faster on foot than I in my black ship?"

Which Pope renders thus :

"O, say, what angry power Elpenor led
To glide in shades, and wander with the dead ?
How could thy soul, by realms and seas disjoined,
Outfly the nimble sail, and leave the lagging wind ?"

I sincerely hope the reader finds no pleasure here, either in the nimbleness of the sail, or the laziness of the wind !   And yet how is it that these conceits are so painful now, when they have been pleasant to us in the other instances?

---

[1] " Well said, Old mole ! can'st work i' the ground so fast ?"

For a very simple reason. They are not a *pathetic* fallacy at all, for they are put into the mouth of the wrong passion—a passion which never could possibly have spoken them—agonized curiosity. Ulysses wants to know the facts of the matter; and the very last thing his mind could do at the moment would be to pause, or suggest in any wise what was *not* a fact. The delay in the first three lines, and conceit in the last, jar upon us instantly, like the most frightful discord in music. No poet of true imaginative power could possibly have written the passage. It is worth while comparing the way a similar question is put by the exquisite sincerity of Keats :

> " He wept, and his bright tears
> Went trickling down the golden bow he held.
> Thus, with half-shut. suffused eyes, he stood ;
> While from beneath some cumb'rous boughs hard by,
> With solemn step, an awful goddess came.
> And there was purport in her looks for him,
> Which he with eager guess began to read :
> Perplexed the while. melodiously he said,
> ' *How cam'st thou over the unfooted sea ?* ' "

Therefore, we see that the spirit of truth must guide us in some sort, even in our enjoyment of fallacy. Coleridge's fallacy has no discord in it, but Pope's has set our teeth on edge. Without farther questioning, I will endeavor to state the main bearings of this matter.

The temperament which admits the pathetic fallacy is, as I said above, that of a mind and body in some sort too weak to deal fully with what is before them or upon them ; borne away, or over-clouded,

or over-dazzled by emotion ; and it is a more or less
noble state, according to the force of the emotion
which has induced it. For it is no credit to a man
that he is not morbid or inaccurate in his perceptions, when he has no strength of feeling to warp
them ; and it is in general a sign of higher capacity
and stand in the ranks of being, that the emotions
should be strong enough to vanquish, partly, the
intellect, and make it believe what they choose. But
it is still a grander condition when the intellect also
rises, till it is strong enough to assert its rule against,
or together with, the utmost efforts of the passions ;
and the whole man stands in an iron glow, white hot,
perhaps, but still strong, and in no wise evaporat-
ing ; even if he melts, losing none of his weight.

So, then, we have the three ranks : the man who
perceives rightly, because he does not feel, and to
whom the primrose is very accurately the primrose,
because he does not love it. Then, secondly, the
man who perceives wrongly, because he feels, and to
whom the primrose is anything else than a primrose :
a star, or a sun, or a fairy's shield, or a forsaken
maiden. And then, lastly, there is the man who
perceives rightly in spite of his feelings, and to whom
the primrose is forever nothing else than itself—a
little flower, apprehended in the very plain and leafy
fact of it, whatever and how many soever the associations and passions may be, that crowd around it.
And, in general, these three classes may be rated in
comparative order, as the men who are not poets at
all, and the poets of the second order, and the poets

of the first ; only however great a man may be, there
are always some subjects which *ought* to throw him
off his balance ; some, by which his poor human
capacity of thought should be conquered, and brought
into the inaccurate and vague state of perception, so
that the language of the highest inspiration becomes
broken, obscure, and wild in metaphor, resembling
that of the weaker man, overborne by weaker
things.

And thus, in full, there are four classes : the men
who feel nothing, and therefore see truly ; the men
who feel strongly, think weakly, and see untruly
(second order of poets) ; the men who feel strongly,
think strongly, and see truly (first order of poets) ;
and the men who, strong as human creatures can be,
are yet submitted to influences stronger than they,
and see in a sort untruly, because what they see is
inconceivably above them. This last is the usual
condition of prophetic inspiration.

I separate these classes, in order that their character may be clearly understood ; but of course they
are united each to the other by imperceptible tran-
sitions, and the same mind, according to the influences to which it is subjected, passes at different
times into the various states. Still, the difference
between the great and less man is, on the whole,
chiefly in this point of *alterability.* That is to say,
the one knows too much, and perceives and feels too
much of the past and future, and of all things beside
and around that which immediately affects him, to
be in any wise shaken by it. His mind is made up ;

his thoughts have an accustomed current; his ways are steadfast; it is not this or that new sight which will at once unbalance him. He is tender to impression at the surface, like a rock with deep moss upon it; but there is too much mass of him to be moved. The smaller man, with the same degree of sensibility, is at once carried off his feet; he wants to do something he did not want to do before; he views all the universe in a new light through his tears; he is gay or enthusiastic, melancholy or passionate, as things come and go to him. Therefore the high creative poet might even be thought, to a great extent, impassive (as shallow people think Dante stern), receiving indeed all feelings to the full, but having a great centre of reflection and knowledge in which he stands serene, and watches the feeling, as it were, from far off.

Dante, in his most intense moods, has entire command of himself, and can look around calmly, at all moments, for the image or the word that will best tell what he sees to the upper or lower world. But Keats and Tennyson, and the poets of the second order, are generally themselves subdued by the feelings under which they write, or, at least, write as choosing to be so, and therefore admit certain expressions and modes of thought which are in some sort diseased or false.

Now so long as we see that the *feeling* is true, we pardon, or are even pleased by, the confessed fallacy of sight which it induces : we are pleased, for instance, with those lines of Kingsley's, above quoted, not

because they fallaciously describe foam, but because
they faithfully describe sorrow. But the moment
the mind of the speaker becomes cold, that moment
every such expression becomes untrue, as being forever untrue in the external facts. And there is no
greater baseness in literature than the habit of using
these metaphorical expressions in cold blood. An
inspired writer, in full impetuosity of passion, may
speak wisely and truly of " raging waves of the sea,
foaming out their own shame ;" but it is only the
basest writer who cannot speak of the sea without
talking of " raging waves," " remorseless floods,"
" ravenous billows," etc.; and it is one of the signs
of the highest power in a writer to check all such
habits of thought, and to keep his eyes fixed firmly
on the *pure fact*, out of which if any feeling comes
to him or his reader, he knows it must be a true
one.

To keep to the waves, I forget who it is who represents a man in despair, desiring that his body may
be cast into the sea,

" *Whose changing mound and foam that passed away,*
Might mock the eye that questioned where I lay."

Observe, there is not a single false, or even over-
charged, expression. " Mound " of the sea wave is
perfectly simple and true ; " changing" is as familiar
as may be ; " foam that passed away," strictly literal ;
and the whole line descriptive of the reality with a
degree of accuracy which I know not any other verse,
in the range of poetry, that altogether equals. For
most people have not a distinct idea of the clumsi-

ness and massiveness of a large wave. The word
"wave" is used too generally of ripples and breakers,
and bendings in light drapery or grass: it does not
by itself convey a perfect image. But the word
"mound" is heavy, large, dark, definite; there is no
mistaking the kind of wave meant, nor missing the
sight of it. Then the term "changing" has a peculiar force also. Most people think of waves as rising
and falling. But if they look at the sea carefully,
they will perceive that the waves do not rise and
fall. They change. Change both place and form,
but they do not fall; one wave goes on, and on, and
still on; now lower, now higher, now tossing its mane
like a horse, now building itself together like a wall,
now shaking, now steady, but still the same wave,
till at last it seems struck by something, and changes,
one knows not how,—becomes another wave.

The close of the line insists on this image, and
paints it still more perfectly,—"foam that passed
away." Not merely melting, disappearing, but passing on, out of sight, on the career of the wave.
Then, having put the absolute ocean fact as far as he
may before our eyes, the poet leaves us to feel about
it as we may, and to trace for ourselves the opposite
fact,—the image of the green mounds that do not
change, and the white and written stones that do not
pass away; and thence to follow out also the associated images of the calm life with the quiet grave,
and the despairing life with the fading foam :—

"Let no man move his bones."
"As for Samaria, her king is cut off like the foam upon the water."

But nothing of this is actually told or pointed out, and the expressions, as they stand, are perfectly severe and accurate, utterly uninfluenced by the firmly governed emotion of the writer. Even the word " mock " is hardly an exception, as it may stand merely for " deceive " or " defeat," without implying any impersonation of the waves.

It may be well, perhaps, to give one or two more instances to show the peculiar dignity possessed by all passages which thus limit their expression to the pure fact, and leave the hearer to gather what he can from it. Here is a notable one from the Iliad. Helen, looking from the Scæan gate of Troy over the Grecian host, and telling Priam the names of its captains, says at last :

" I see all the other dark-eyed Greeks ; but two I cannot see,—Castor and Pollux,—whom one mother bore with me. Have they not followed from fair Lacedæmon, or have they indeed come in their sea-wandering ships, but now will not enter into the battle of men, fearing the shame and the scorn that is in me ?"

Then Homer :

" So she spoke. But them, already, the life-giving earth possessed, there in Lacedæmon, in the dear fatherland."

Note, here, the high poetical truth carried to the extreme. The poet has to speak of the earth in sadness, but he will not let that sadness affect or change his thoughts of it. No ; though Castor and Pollux be dead, yet the earth is our mother still, fruitful, life-giving. These are the facts of the thing.

I see nothing else than these.   Make what you will
of them.[1]

—— Now in this there is the exact type of the
consummate poetical temperament.   For, be it
clearly and constantly remembered, that the greatness of a poet depends upon the two faculties, acuteness of feeling, and command of it.   A poet is great,
first in proportion to the strength of his passion, and
then, that strength being granted, in proportion to
his government of it ; there being, however, always
a point beyond which it would be inhuman and
monstrous if he pushed this government, and, therefore, a point at which all feverish and wild fancy becomes just and true.   Thus the destruction of the
kingdom of Assyria cannot be contemplated firmly
by a prophet of Israel.   The fact is too great, too
wonderful.   It overthrows him, dashes him into a
confused element of dreams.   All the world is, to his
stunned thought, full of strange voices.   " Yea, the
fir-trees rejoice at thee, and the cedars of Lebanon,
saying, ' Since thou art gone down to the grave, no
feller has come up against us.' "   So, still more, the
thought of the presence of Deity cannot be borne
without this great astonishment.   " The mountains

---

[1] [This paragraph is criticised by Matthew Arnold (*On Translating
Homer*, p. 148): " This is a just specimen of that sort of application
of modern sentiment to the ancients against which a student who
wishes to feel the ancients truly cannot too resolutely defend himself. . . It is not true, as a matter of general criticism, that this kind
of sentimentality, eminently modern, inspires Homer at all."]

and the hills shall break forth before you into singing, and all the trees of the fields shall clap their
hands."

But by how much this feeling is noble when it is
justified by the strength of its cause, by so much it
is ignoble when there is not cause enough for it; and
beyond all other ignobleness is the mere affectation
of it, in hardness of heart. Simply bad writing may
almost always, as above noticed, be known by its
adoption of these fanciful metaphorical expressions,
as a sort of current coin; yet there is even a worse,
at least a more harmful, condition of writing than
this, in which such expressions are not ignorantly
and feelinglessly caught up, but, by some master,
skilful in handling, yet insincere, deliberately wrought
out with chill and studied fancy; as if we should try
to make an old lava stream look red-hot again by
covering it with dead leaves, or white-hot, with hoar-
frost.

When Young is lost in veneration, as he dwells on
the character of a truly good and holy man, he permits himself for a moment to be overborne by the
feeling so far as to exclaim—

" Where shall I find him? angels, tell me where.
You know him; he is near you; point him out.
Shall I see glories beaming from his brow,
Or trace his footsteps by the rising flowers?"

This emotion has a worthy cause, and is thus true
and right. But now hear the cold-hearted Pope say
to a shepherd girl—

" Where'er you walk, cool gales shall fan the glade !
   Trees, where you sit, shall crowd into a shade ;
   Your praise the birds shall chant in every grove,
   And winds shall waft it to the powers above.
   But would you sing, and rival Orpheus' strain,
   The wondering forests soon should dance again;
   The moving mountain hear the powerful call,
   And headlong streams hang, listening, in their fall."

This is not, nor could it for a moment be mistaken
for, the language of passion.   It is simple falsehood,
uttered by hypocrisy ; definite absurdity, rooted in
affectation, and coldly asserted in the teeth of nature
and fact.   Passion will indeed go far in deceiving
itself ; but it must be a strong passion, not the simple
wish of a lover to tempt his mistress to sing.   Compare a very closely parallel passage in Wordsworth,
in which the lover has lost his mistress :

" Three years had Barbara in her grave been laid,
   When thus his moan he made:
 ' Oh, move, thou cottage, from behind yon oak,
    Or let the ancient tree uprooted lie,
   That in some other way yon smoke
    May mount into the sky.

" If still behind yon pine-tree's ragged bough,
    Headlong, the water-fall must come,
    Oh, let it, then, be dumb—
   Be anything, sweet stream, but that which thou art now.' "

Here is a cottage to be moved, if not a mountain,
and a water-fall to be silent, if it is not to hang listening ; but with what different relation to the mind
that contemplates them !   Here, in the extremity of
its agony, the soul cries out wildly for relief, which at

the same moment it partly knows to be impossible,
but partly believes possible, in a vague impression
that a miracle *might* be wrought to give relief even
to a less sore distress,—that nature is kind, and God
is kind, and that grief is strong; it knows not well
what *is* possible to such grief. To silence a stream,
to move a cottage wall,—one might think it could
do as much as that!

RICHARD HOLT HUTTON.

1826–

. [Mr. Hutton is the author of some of the most thoughtful
and appreciative literary essays of the generation. He writes
with fine artistic as well as intellectual judgment, and is especially marked by his sympathetic interpretation of the
ethical and spiritual values of literature. The passage that
follows is from the essay on Cardinal Newman, in his " Modern Guides of English Thought in Matters of Faith." This
volume, and that entitled " Literary Essays," contain his
more important critical studies.]

**From the Essay on Cardinal Newman, in " Modern Guides to
English Thought in Matters of Faith."**

MOST of us know, by bust, photograph, or picture,
the wonderful face of the great Cardinal ; '—that
wide forehead, ploughed deep with parallel horizon-
tal furrows which seem to express his careworn
grasp of the double aspect of human nature, its aspect in the intellectual and its aspect in the spiritual
world,—the pale cheek down which

> "long lines of shadow slope
> Which years, and curious thought, and suffering give,"

—the pathetic eye, which speaks compassion from
afar, and yet gazes wonderingly into the impassable
gulf which separates man from man,—and the strange

[' John Henry, Cardinal Newman.]

mixture of asceticism and tenderness in all the lines
of that mobile and reticent mouth, where humor,
playfulness, and sympathy are intricately blended
with those severer moods that " refuse and restrain."
On the whole, it is a face full, in the first place, of spiritual passion of the highest order, and in the next, of
that subtle and intimate knowledge of details of
human limitation and weakness which makes all
spiritual passion look utterly ambitious and hopeless
unless indeed it be guided amongst the stakes and
dikes and pitfalls of the human battlefield by the
direct providence of God.

And not a little of what I say of Cardinal Newman's countenance may be said also of his style. A
great French critic has declared that "style *is* the
man." But surely that cannot be asserted without
qualification. There are some styles which are much
better than the man, through failing to reflect the
least admirable parts of him ; and many that are
much worse—for example, styles affected by the artificial influence of conventional ideas like those which
prevailed in the last century. Again, there are styles
which are thoroughly characteristic of the man in
one sense, and yet are characteristic in part because
they show his delight in viewing both himself and
the universe through colored media, which, while
they brilliantly represent some aspects of it, greatly
misrepresent or completely disguise all others. Such
a style was Carlyle's, who may be said to have seen
the universe with wonderful vividness as it was when
in earthquake and hurricane, but not to have appre-

hended at all that solid crust of earth symbolizing the conventional phlegmatic nature which most of us know only too well. Gibbon, again, sees everything—even himself—as if it were a striking pageant. How characteristically he describes his father's disapprobation of his youthful passion for Mademoiselle Curchod (afterwards Madame Necker): "I sighed as a lover, I obeyed as a son!" It was evidently the moral pageant of that very mild ardor, and that not too reluctant submission, of which he was thinking, not of the emotion itself. And Macaulay, again, has a style like a coat of mail with the visor down. It is burnished, brilliant, imposing; but it presents the world and human life in pictorial antitheses far more vivid and brilliant than real. It is a style which effectually conceals all the more homely domestic aspects of Macaulay's own nature, and represents mainly his hunger for incisive contrast. But if ever it were true that the style is the man, it is true, I think, of Newman—nay, of both Newman and Matthew Arnold. And therefore I may venture without impropriety to dwell somewhat longer on the style of both, and especially of the former, than would be ordinarily justifiable. Both styles are luminous, both are marked by that curious "distinction" which only genius, and in general only poetic genius, can command. Both show a great delight in irony, and use it with great effect. Both writers can, when they choose, indulge even in extravagance, and give the rein to ridicule without rousing that displeasure which any such excess in men of high intel-

lectual power is apt to excite. Both styles are
styles of white light rather than of lurid, or glowing, or even rainbow order. Both, in poetry at
least, and Newman's in both poetry and prose, are
capable of expressing the truest kind of pathos.
Both have something in them of the older Oxford
suavity, though in very different forms. I have
heard it said that the characteristic Oxford manner
is " ostentatiously sweet," as the characteristic Cam-
bridge manner is ostentatiously clumsy. But neither
Cardinal Newman nor Matthew Arnold have the
slightest trace of this excess of suavity, of the *eau
sucrée* attributed to the university. Newman's sweetness is the sweetness of religious humility and ardor,
Arnold's is the sweetness of easy condescension.
Newman's sweetness is wistful, Arnold is didactic ;
the one yearns to move your heart, the other kindly
enlightens your intellect. Even Newman's prose
style is spiritual in its basis, Arnold's intellectual.
Even when treating spiritual topics, even when saying the best things Arnold has ever said as to " the
secret of Jesus," his manner, though gracious, is gently dictatorial. Again, when Newman gives the rein
to his irony, it is always with a certain earnestness
or even indignation against the self-deceptions he is
ridiculing. When Arnold does so, it is in pleasurable
scorn of the folly he is exposing.

——Both are luminous, but Arnold's prose is luminous like a steel mirror, Newman's like a clear at-

mosphere or lake. Arnold's prose style is crystal, Newman's liquid.

And with this indication of the characteristic difference I will now turn to my immediate subject, Cardinal Newman's style only. It is a style, as I have said, that more nearly represents a clear atmosphere than any other which I know in English literature. It flows round you, it presses gently on every side of you, and yet like a steady current carries you in one direction too. On every facet of your mind and heart you feel the light touch of his purpose, and yet you cannot escape the general drift of his movement more than the ship can escape the drift of the tide. He never said anything more characteristic than when he expressed his conviction that, though there are a hundred difficulties in faith, into all of which he could enter, the hundred difficulties are not equivalent to a single doubt. That saying is most characteristic even of his style, which seems to be sensitive in the highest degree to a multitude of hostile influences which are at once appreciated and resisted, while one predominant and over-ruling power moves steadily on.

I will try and illustrate my meaning briefly. Take the following passage concerning the lower animals:

"Can anything be more marvellous or startling, unless we were used to it, than that we should have a race of beings about us whom we do see, and as little know their state, or can describe their interests or their destiny, as we can tell of the inhabitants of the sun and moon? It is, indeed, a very over-

powering thought, when we get to fix our minds on
it, that we periodically use—I may say hold intercourse with—creatures who are as much strangers
to us, as mysterious, as if they were fabulous un-
earthly beings, more powerful than man, and yet
his slaves, which Eastern superstitions have invented. We have more real knowledge about the
angels than about brutes ; they have apparently pas
sions, habits, and a certain accountableness, but all
is mystery about them. We do not know whether
they can sin or not, whether they are under punish-
ment, whether they are to live after this life ; we inflict
very great sufferings on a portion of them, and they,
in turn, every now and then, retaliate upon us, as if
by a wonderful law. . . . Cast your thoughts abroad
on the whole number of them, large and small, in
vast forests, or in the water, or in the air, and then
say whether the presence of such countless multitudes, so various in their natures, so strange and
wild in their shapes, living on the earth without
ascertainable object, is not as mysterious as anything Scripture says about the angels."

Now, does not the style of that passage perfectly
represent the character of mind which conceived it,
as well as the special meaning it conveys ? Inferior
styles express the purpose but conceal the man ;
Newman's expresses the purpose by revealing the
man. This passage—and I could find scores which
would suit my purpose as well, and some, though not
so short and detachable, that would suit it better—
is as luminous as the day ; but that is not its special

characteristic, for luminousness belongs to the ether,
which is the same whether the atmosphere be present or absent, and Newman's style touches you with
a visible thrill, just as the atmosphere transmits
every vibration of sound. You are conscious of the
thrill of the writer's spirit as he contemplates this
strange world of countless animated beings with
whom our spiritual bond is so slight; the sufferings
we inflict, and the retaliations permitted in return;
the blindness to spiritual marvels with which custom
strikes us; the close analogy between the genii of
Eastern superstition and the domestic animals who
serve us so industriously with physical powers so
much greater than our own; the strangeness and
wildness of the innumerable forms which hover
round us in forest, field, and flood; and yet with all
those undercurrents of feeling, observe how large is
the imaginative reach of the whole; how firmly the
drift—to make it easier to believe in angelic hosts—
is sustained; how steady is the subordination of the
whole to the object of attenuating the difficulty of
the spiritual mystery in which he desires men to
believe. Once more, how tender is the style in the
only sense in which we can properly attribute tenderness to style, its avoidance of every harsh or
violent word, its shrinking aside from anything like
overstatement! The lower animals have, he says,
" apparently passions, habits, and a certain accountableness." Evidently Dr. Newman could not have
suggested, as Descartes did, that they are machines
aping feelings without having them; he never

doubts their sufferings; he could not, even by a
shade, exaggerate the mystery he is delineating.
Every touch shows that he wishes to delineate it as
it is, and not to overcolor it by a single tint. Then
how piercing to our dulness is that phrase, " It is
indeed a very overpowering thought, *when we get to
fix our minds on it.*" We are not overpowered, he
would say, only because we cannot or do not fix our
minds on this wonderful intercourse of ours with
intimates after a kind, of whose inner being we are
yet entirely ignorant. And how reticent is the inference, how strictly it limits itself to its real object,
to impress upon us how little we know even of the
objects of sense, and how little reason there is in
using our ignorance as the standard by which to
measure the supersensual !

——And now to bring to a close what I have to say
of Dr. Newman's style—though the subject grows
upon one—let me quote one or two of the passages
in which his style vibrates to the finest notes, and
yet exhibits most powerfully the drift and undercurrent by which his mind is swayed. Perhaps he never
expresses anything so powerfully as he expresses
the deep pining for the rest of spiritual simplicity, for
the peace which passes understanding, that under-
lies his nature. Take this from one of his Roman
Catholic sermons: "Oh, long sought after, tardily
found, the desire of the eyes, the joy of the heart,
the truth after many shadows, the fulness after many
foretastes, the home after many storms; come to

her, poor children, for she it is, and she alone, who
can unfold to you the secret of your being, and the
meaning of your destiny." Again, in the exquisite
tale of martyrdom from which I have already quoted
the account of the locusts, the destined martyr,
whose thirst for God has been awakened by her
intercourse with Christians, thus repels the Greek
rhetorician who is trying to feed her on the husks
of philosophic abstractions, as she expresses the
yearnings of a heart weary of its desolation : "Oh
that I could find Him !" Callista exclaimed passionately. "On the right hand and on the left I grope,
but touch Him not. Why dost thou fight against
me, why dost thou scare and perplex me, O First
and only fair ?"

——In another of these poems Dr. Newman has
referred to the sea described in the book of Reve-
lation :

> " A sea before
> The throne is spread ; its pure still glass
> Pictures all earth-scenes as they pass.
> We on its shore
> Share in the bosom of our rest,
> God's knowledge, and are blest."

It has always seemed to me that Newman's style
succeeds, so far as a human form of expression can,
in picturing the feelings of earth in a medium as
clear, as liquid, and as tranquil, as sensitive alike to
the minutest ripples and the most potent tidal waves
of providential impulse, as the sea spread before the
throne itself.

WALTER PATER.

1839–

[This extract from Mr. Pater's essay on Style, contained in his volume of literary studies entitled " Appreciations," puts in a noteworthy way the importance of perfect language for art's sake. A passage of similar import has already been given, but the subject is treated here with more detail, and the sense for expression is so essential to intelligent literary enjoyment that a second presentation of it is not superfluous. The faculty for recognizing and feeling the values of words on both the intellectual and artistic sides—nice discrimination in meaning, and æsthetic tact in verbal tone and sentence rhythm, is one of the later and more acquired literary refinements, and more than repays attention and study. The only danger in this connection is the possibility both for writers and for readers of a cold and cramping fastidiousness. When too much stress is thrown on exquisite verbal effect, there is danger of a cautiously critical, if not self-conscious tone. Perhaps Mr. Pater's own writings have occasionally a studied look, as if they had been polished with one file too many. The accidents of genius are often felicitous beyond studious correctness. The unexpected word, which formal theory might not always indorse, is sometimes the poetry of verbal selection that study can never attain. But the ordinary danger is in neglecting such admonitions as these upon the importance of finish and precision, whether in what we compose, or in attending to the work of others. Not a little of the cultivated reader's gratification in reading, is his perception of the beauties of artistic workmanship.]

From the Essay on Style, in "Appreciations."

——Just in proportion as the writer's aim, consciously or unconsciously, comes to be the transcribing, not of the world, not of mere fact, but of his sense of it, he becomes an artist, his work *fine* art; and good art in proportion to the truth of his presentment of that sense ; as in those humbler or plainer functions of literature also, truth—truth to bare fact, there—is the essence of such artistic quality as they may have.   Truth ! there can be no merit, no craft at all, without that.   And further, all beauty is in the long run only *fineness* of truth, or what we call expression, the finer accommodation of speech to that vision within.

The transcript of his sense of fact, rather than the fact, as being preferable, pleasanter, more beautiful to the writer himself.   In literature as in every other product of human skill, in the moulding of a bell or a platter, for instance, wherever this sense asserts itself, wherever the producer so modifies his work as, over and above its primary use or intention, to make it pleasing (to himself, of course, in the first instance), there "fine" as opposed to merely serviceable art exists.   Literary art, that is, like all art which is in any way imitative or reproductive of fact—form, or color, or incident—is the representation of such fact as connected with soul, of a specific personality, in its preferences, its volition and power.

——The literary artist is of necessity a scholar, and in what he professes to do will have in mind,

first of all, the scholar and the scholarly conscience
—the male conscience in this matter, as we must think
it, under a system of education which still to so large
an extent limits real scholarship to men.   In his self-
criticism he supposes always that sort of reader who
will go (full of eyes) warily, considerately, though without consideration for him, over the ground which the
female conscience traverses so lightly, so amiably.
For the material in which he works is no more a creation of his own than the sculptor's marble. Product of
a myriad various minds and contending tongues, compact of obscure and minute association, a language
has its own abundant and often recondite laws, in
the habitual and summary recognition of which
scholarship consists.   A writer full of a matter he is
before all things anxious to express, may think of
those laws, the limitations of vocabulary, structure,
and the like, as a restriction, but if a real artist will
find in them an opportunity.   His punctilious observance of the proprieties of his medium will diffuse
through all he writes a general air of sensibility, of
refined usage.   *Exclusiones debitæ naturæ*—the ex-
clusions, or rejections, which nature demands—we
know how large a part these play, according to
Bacon, in the science of nature. In a somewhat
changed sense, we might say that the art of the
scholar is summed up in the observance of those rejections demanded by the nature of his medium,
the material he must use. Alive to the value of an
atmosphere in which every term finds its utmost degree of expression, and with all the jealousy of a

lover of words, he will resist a constant tendency on the part of the majority of those who use them to efface the distinction of language, the facility of writers often reinforcing in this respect the work of the vulgar. He will feel the obligation not of the laws only, but of those affinities, avoidances, those mere preferences of his language, which through the associations of literary history have become a part of its nature, prescribing the rejection of many a neology, many a license, many a gypsy phrase which might present itself as actually expressive. His appeal, again, is to the scholar, who has great experience in literature, and will show no favor to short cuts, or hackneyed illustration, or an affectation of learning designed for the unlearned. Hence a contention, a sense of self-restraint and renunciation, having for the susceptible reader the effect of a challenge for minute consideration ; the attention of the writer, in every minutest detail, being a pledge that it is worth the reader's while to be attentive too, that the writer is dealing scrupulously with his instrument, and therefore, indirectly, with the reader himself also, that he has the science of the instrument he plays on, perhaps, after all, with a freedom which in such case will be the freedom of the master.

——If all high things have their martyrs, Gustave Flaubert might perhaps rank as the martyr of literary style. In his printed correspondence a curious series of letters, written in his twenty-fifth year, records what seems to have been his one other passion

—a series of letters which, with its fine casuistries,
its firmly repressed anguish, its tone of harmonious
grey, and the sense of disillusion in which the whole
matter ends, might have been, a few slight changes
supposed, one of his own fictions.

" I must scold you," he writes, " for one thing, which shocks,
scandalizes me—the small concern, namely, you show for art
just now. As regards glory be it so : there, I approve. But
for art!—the one thing in life that is good and real—can you
compare with it an earthly love? prefer the adoration of a
relative beauty to the *cultus* of the true beauty? Well! I tell
you the truth. That is the one thing good in me: the one
thing I have, to me estimable. For yourself, you blend with
the beautiful a heap of alien things, the useful, the agreeable,
what not?—

"The only way not to be unhappy is to shut yourself up
in art, and count everything else as nothing. Pride takes
the place of all beside when it is established on a large basis.
Work! God wills it. That, it seems to me, is clear.—

" I am reading over again the Æneid, certain verses of
which I repeat to myself to satiety. There are phrases there
which stay in one's head, by which I find myself beset, as
with those musical airs which are forever returning and cause
you pain, you love them so much. I observe that I no
longer laugh much and am no longer depressed. I am ripe.
You talk of my serenity and envy me. It may well surprise
you. Sick, irritated, the prey a thousand times a day of
cruel pain, I continue my labor like a true working-man,
who, with sleeves turned up, in the sweat of his brow,
beats away at his anvil, never troubling himself whether it
rains or blows, for hail or thunder. I was not like that
formerly. The change has taken place naturally, though
my will has counted for something in the matter.—

" Those who write in good style are sometimes accused of
a neglect of ideas, and of the moral end, as if the end of the

physician were something else than healing, of the painter
than painting—as if the end of art were not, before all else,
the beautiful."

What, then, did Flaubert understand by beauty,
in the art he pursued with so much fervor, with so
much self-command? Let us hear a sympathetic
commentator :—

" Possessed of an absolute belief that there exists but one
way of expressing one thing, one word to call it by, one adjective to qualify, one verb to animate it, he gave himself
to superhuman labor for the discovery, in every phrase, of
that word, that verb, that epithet. In this way, he believed
in some mysterious harmony of expression, and when a
true word seemed to him to lack euphony still went on seek-
ing another, with invincible patience, certain that he had not
yet got hold of the unique word. . . . A thousand preoccu-
pations would beset him at the same moment, always with
this desperate certitude fixed in his spirit: Among all the
expressions in the world, all forms and turns of expression,
there is but *one*—one form, one mode—to express what I
want to say."

The one word for the one thing, the one thought,
amid the multitude of words, terms, that might just
do: the problem of style was there !—the unique
word, phrase, sentence, paragraph, essay, or song,
absolutely proper to the single mental presentation
or vision within. In that perfect justice, over and
above the many contingent and removable beauties
with which beautiful style may charm us, but which
it can exist without, independent of them yet dex-
terously availing itself of them, omnipresent in good
work, in function at every point, from single epithets

to the rhythm of a whole book, lay the specific, indispensable, very intellectual, beauty of literature,
the possibility of which constitutes it a fine art.

One seems to detect the influence of a philosophic
idea there—the idea of a natural economy, of some
pre-existent adaptation, between a relative, somewhere in the world of thought and its correlative,
somewhere in the world of language—both alike,
rather, somewhere in the mind of the artist, deside-
rative, expectant, inventive—meeting each other with
the readiness of " soul and body reunited " in Blake's
rapturous design ; and, in fact, Flaubert was fond of
giving his theory philosophical expression.

" There are no beautiful thoughts," he would say, " without beautiful forms, and conversely. As it is impossible to
extract from a physical body the qualities which really constitute it—color, extension, and the like—without reducing
it to a hollow abstraction, in a word, without destroying it ;
just so it is impossible to detach the form from the idea, for
the idea only exists by virtue of the form,"

All the recognized flowers, the removable ornaments of literature (including harmony and ease in
reading aloud, very carefully considered by him),
counted, certainly ; for these too are part of the
actual value of what one says. But still, after all,
with Flaubert, the search, the unwearied research, was
not for the smooth, or winsome, or forcible word, as
such, as with false Ciceronians, but quite simply and
honestly, for the word's adjustment to its meaning.
The first condition of this must be, of course, to
know yourself, to have ascertained your own sense

exactly. Then, if we suppose an artist, he says to the reader,—I want you to see precisely what I see. Into the mind sensitive to " form" a flood of random sounds, colors, incidents, is ever penetrating from the world without, to become, by sympathetic selection, a part of its very structure, and, in turn, the visible vesture and expression of that other world it sees so steadily within, nay, already with a partial conformity thereto, to be refined, enlarged, corrected, at a hundred points; and it is just there, just at those doubtful points, that the function of style as tact or taste, intervenes.

——In this way, according to the well-known saying, " The style is the man," complex or simple, in his individuality, his plenary sense of what he really has to say, his sense of the world; all cautions regarding style arising out of so many natural scruples as to the medium through which alone he can expose that inward sense of things, the purity of this medium, its laws or tricks of refraction : nothing is to be left there which might give conveyance to any matter save that.   Style in all its varieties, reserved or opulent, terse, abundant, musical, stimulant, academic, so long as each is really characteristic or expressive, finds thus its justification, the sumptuous good taste of Cicero being as truly the man himself, and not another, justified, yet insured inalienably to him, thereby, as would have been his portrait by Raffaelle, in full consular splendor, on his ivory chair.

NOTES.

THESE topical analyses and suggestions are designed for the use of students—not of teachers. The editor has learned by experience that many read passages assigned for study without seeming able to derive distinct impressions of the leading ideas, and also without developing the full meaning of many brief or allusive expressions, or following out principles and views to their consequences, and making them distinct by definite illustration. The pages that follow will perhaps aid in focusing the attention and stimulating the thought of those to whom much æsthetic criticism is difficult. They are by no means intended to be exhaustive, either as topics of the text or as hints for reflection. The few points in the text that appear to require explanation will be noticed in connection with these other suggestions.

SIR PHILIP SIDNEY.

The elements in Sidney's conception of poetry.

Expressions that illustrate his ideal spirit;—his poetic feeling.

His contrast between poetry and philosophy.

The instructive element in poetry. [Is this synonymous with didactic?]

Sidney's figures and illustrations,—homely; poetical; their ease, and aptness.

The contrast between the diction of prose and poetry.

Sidney's idea of the secondary and the final aims of learning.

His style—the secret of its charm. Its defect, from a modern standpoint.

Personal traits suggested ; marks of humor ; his literary studies.

BEN JONSON.

The relation of diction to character. Comparison of Sidney and Jonson by this test. [Cp. Spenser's Platonic line, at the end of the Introduction.] Modifications of the view. Illustrations from such authors as Wordsworth, Carlyle, and Arnold. [Cp. p. 195.]   .

Jonson's deference to classical literature; its conservatism ; reasonableness.

Touch of the aristocrat of genius in his remarks on critics. The aim of criticism.

Parallel between Jonson and the extract from Sidney.

The ethical in Jonson's notion of poetry. [Cp. Prologue to the Alchemist, e.g., or the Dedication of Volpone : " The end of poesie is to inform men in the best reason of living."]

Jonson's conception of the literary artist.

His estimate of the excellence of untrained spontaneity.

The artist's ambition respecting passages, and his work as a whole. His sacrifices and reward.

Constituents of literary success. Is this standard of taste strictly English ? [Jonson's sensitiveness to his reputation of requiring time and effort for writing well, disposed him to a severe judgment of his more careless contemporaries. The implied estimate of Marlowe in the reference to " Tamerlane" is no more fair than gracious to the great early dramatist. Jonson was so much more of a realist than Marlowe that he loses sight of the latter's superb passages, in view of their epic rather than dramatic genius, and the over-heroic unreality of most of his characterization. It is unjust to take as a type of the strutting and vociferation of

the pre-Shakespearean stage a play which contains such
lines as,

> Our souls, whose faculties can comprehend
> The wondrous architecture of the world,
> And measure every wandering planet's course,
> Still climbing after knowledge infinite,
> And always moving as the restless spheres ;   *Tamerlane*

or the simile beginning,

> As when the seaman sees the Hyades
> Gather an army of Cimmerian clouds.]

The aim of style.

Jonson's different propositions about the use of words.
His scholarly exclusiveness.

Reiteration of earlier warning. Precise force of his most
poetical illustration.

Honorable assistance from other authors. What should
determine choice of style? Practical suggestions for composition.

Examples of Jonson's sententious expression. Advantage
of old words. Basis for the remark on the parts of composition to be most regarded. In what does the difficulty (if
any) in Jonson's manner consist?

With the passage on uses of words, it is profitable to compare Horace, *Ars Poetica* (near the beginning), and Lowell's
Introduction to the Biglow Papers, from which a few sentences may be extracted : " It had long seemed to me that
the great vice of American writing and speaking was a studied want of simplicity, that we were in danger of coming to
look on our mother-tongue as a dead language, to be sought
in the grammar and dictionary rather than in the heart. . . .
It is only from its roots in the living generations of men
that a language can be reinforced with fresh vigor for its
needs ; what may be called a literate dialect grows ever
more and more pedantic and foreign, till it becomes at last
as unfitting a vehicle for living thought as monkish Latin.

That we should all be made to talk like books is the danger
with which we are threatened by the Universal Schoolmaster.
. . . No language after it has faded into *diction*, none that
cannot suck up the feeding juices secreted for it in the rich
mother-earth of common folk, can bring forth a sound and
lusty book. . . .

" But while the schoolmaster has been busy starching our
language and smoothing it flat with the mangle of a supposed classical authority, the newspaper reporter has been
doing even more harm by stretching and swelling it to suit
his occasions. (E.g., 'was hanged' is replaced by 'was
launched into eternity'; 'when the halter was put round his
neck' = 'when the fatal noose was adjusted about the neck
of the unfortunate victim of his own unbridled passions;'
'a great crowd came to see' = 'a vast concourse was as-
sembled to witness,' etc.) . . . I would not be supposed
to condemn truly imaginative prose. There is a simplicity
of splendor, no less than of plainness, and prose would be
poor indeed if it could not find a tongue for that meaning
of the mind which is behind the meaning of the words. It
has sometimes seemed to me that in England there was a
growing tendency to curtail language into a mere conven-
ience, and to defecate it of all emotion as thoroughly as al-
gebraic signs." The entire passage is a strong criticism on
style, aside from the point suggested by the ideas in the
text.

JOHN DRYDEN.

Suggestion as to Dryden's being a careful workman. [Cp.
Dr. Johnson's remarks on p. 44.]

Dryden's opinion of Milton. [Inquire into Milton's reputation at the time.]

Dryden's art in compliment: [—something for which he
was famous, and which he sometimes carried to great ex-
cesses of flattery.]

His conception of criticism. Compare the correctness of

a punctilious, with a more general, standard of excellence. Dryden's own literary method [suggested by his remarks].

Contrast Dryden and Jonson, as to "correctness" of writing, compared with more careless spontaneity.

Examples of Dryden's easy animation of manner.

Apply Dryden's paraphrase from Longinus to the rhetorically inexact figures of speech in *Macbeth*; e.g., such as those in Act I, scene 7. [What later paragraph applies to such a scene?] Compare Shakespeare there, with Jonson. Compare Dryden himself, as in *Annus Mirabilis*.

Dryden's standards of taste among authors.

His view of the aim of poetry in general.

Opinions in which Dryden proves himself above the poetical tendencies of his age.

Discuss the statement that a critic of any given form of literature should sympathize with it.

The degree of force in Dryden's deference to the authority of the past in matters of taste.

A requisite beyond poetry for the best poets.

"Shakespeare knew nothing about 'tropes' and 'metonymies' and 'hyperboles': then why should his readers?" —Dryden's criticism of the principle involved.

The rules of criticism are the practice of the best writers. Defend and illustrate.

Dryden's least defensible examples of strong imagery.

How far is sympathetic feeling for poetry open to imaginative illusion? Illustrate from any poem.

Generalize the defence by Longinus of the hyperbole quoted from Herodotus.

Generalize the principle of Horace's "Si vis me flere," etc.

What requisite for the successful dramatic imitation of the confused language of excitement?

Dryden's coinage of a word.

Enlarge on the definition of poetic license, and illustrate. The effect on many prose writers of a strict application of this principle.

What implied criticism of Paradise Lost? Remark on the motive of its indirectness.

Fault in Tasso and Camoens. [Observe the deeper tendencies that this illustrates in the Revival of Learning.]

Unity of treatment.

Definition of wit. [Distinguish from humor: trace etymological suggestions for each word.]

Basis in nature for figurative writing in passages of strong feeling.

Suggestions about Dryden personally, from his prose style.

Remark upon his vocabulary, illustrations, and sentences.

JOSEPH ADDISON.

Addison's tests for discovering whether one possesses taste.

How far and in what manner taste may be cultivated.

Implied criticism of usual habits of reading.

Addison's conservatism. Personal and original taste—how far recognized. How far should it be?

Contrast Dryden's views on imaginative writing with the tone of Addison here.

Definition of taste, and illustrations.

Recognition of style, essential to literary excellence.

Summarize the most suggestive remarks.

JONATHAN SWIFT.

Momus, a Greek personification of unfavorable judgment, is meant by Swift to express the "patron of the moderns" in their conflict with the classics.

Comment on the allegory. [Hybris, personification of insolent violence; Zoilus, a Greek scholar, who from his criticism on Homer became a type of censoriousness; Tygellius, a literary fault-finder commemorated by Horace. Stymphalus was an Arcadian district whose troublesome birds were destroyed by Hercules.]

Swift's application of the etymological force of the word "critic."

Remark upon "Critics invented rules." Cp. with Dryden's account of the origin of critical precepts.

Swift's ironical explanation of the badness of the writings of his third class of critics.

SAMUEL JOHNSON.

FROM THE LIFE OF POPE.

Definition of genius.

Contrast between Pope and Dryden as to age in beginning literary work. (Annus Mirabilis, 1667 ; Pastorals, 1709; Essay on Criticism, 1711.)

Points where Dryden is Pope's superior. Points where Pope excels. [Write out a list of these and select illustrations from the authors' works.

Johnson's rhetorical power in this passage ; its character. Where most striking ?

To which (Dryden or Pope) does he seem to try more carefully to be fair?

What inference respecting Dr. Johnson's own mental characteristics is justified by these two literary estimates ?

FROM THE LIFE OF COWLEY.

Distinction between verse and poetry.

Compare with Dryden's definition of wit, Pope's and Johnson's.

Summary of the main traits of Cowley's school of poets.

The essential error in their conception of poetry.

Meaning of "uniformity of sentiment :" its service to the writer.

Compare with Johnson's remarks this sonnet of Sidney's :

Loving in truth, and fain in verse my love to show,
  That she, dear she, might take some pleasure of my pain,—
Pleasure might cause her read, reading might make her know,
  Knowledge might pity win and pity grace obtain,—
I sought fit words to paint the blackest face of woe;
  Studying inventions fine, her wits to entertain,
Oft turning others' leaves, to see if thence would flow
  Some fresh and fruitful showers upon my sun-burn'd brain.
But words came halting forth, wanting Invention's stay;
  Invention, Nature's child, fled step-dame Study's blows;
And others' feet still seem'd but strangers in my way.
  Thus, great with child to speak, and helpless in my throes,
Biting my truant pen, beating myself for spite,—
Fool, said my Muse to me, look in thy heart, and write.

Johnson's account of the sublime (note the adjective for his second effect), and the methods of attaining it.

His enumeration of literary faults, outside of these of the "metaphysical poets."

Dr. Johnson does some injustice to the real poetic feeling of such poets as Donne or Jonson. His sense of "the harmony of our numbers" is after the modulation of Denham and Waller, which consists largely in smoothness and technical form. Milton's early poem on Shakespeare and the Nativity ode also have a trace of the style of "conceits."

Dr. Johnson made a large collection of instances of this "metaphysical style," which he prefaces with the observation that "critical remarks are not easily understood without examples." The following will serve to illustrate :

By every wind that comes this way,
  Send me at least a sigh or two,
Such and so many I'll repay,
  As shall themselves make winds to get to you.

Hither with crystal vials, lovers, come,
  And take my tears, which are love's wine,
And try your mistress' tears at home;
  For all are false that taste not just like mine.

Woe to her stubborn heart, if once mine come
Into the self-same room;
'Twill tear and blow up all within,
Like a grenado shot within a magazine.

WILLIAM WORDSWORTH.

Aim of Wordsworth's poetry as to the "essential passions and elementary feelings." Meaning of the expression.

The work to be done by the imagination, in his conception of the Lyrical Ballads.

Advantages to a poet in the choice of rustic and common life.

Wordsworth's contrast between "literary" language and that of humble life.

What modification would Wordsworth make of the latter?

The two main requirements in a poet.

Literary influence of triviality and meanness compared with false refinement. Illustrate these qualities.

Why habits of deep thought involve at least an unconscious purpose in every poem.

"The feeling gives importance to the action and situation." Enlarge and illustrate.

The modern tendency to strong sensations. Enlarge on this, and its results.

The mind's capability of pleasure in quiet ways.

Personification of abstract ideas. (Remark upon the basis of the impulse, and the essentials to its success.)

The meaning and consequences of an author's "looking steadily at his subject."

Why a poet should omit words and images in themselves good.

Enlarge on Wordsworth's remark about good sense.

Point out the conventional marks in Gray's sonnet (cp. the close of the extract from Coleridge.)

[On the contrasts between poetry and painting, read Lessing's Laocoön.]

In what the distinction consists between prose and poetry.

The poet's various characteristics. [What, if any, poetical endowments are omitted here? What sort of personal temperament is suggested by this analysis?]

The false beauty in eighteenth-century literature: its imagery.

Illustrate "a continuous undercurrent of feeling," compared with separate excitements, in our admiration of an author. Generalize the two kinds of literary effect.

[Wordsworth and Coleridge were neighbors at Alfoxden and Nether Stowey, in 1797-8.]

Two cardinal points of poetry. Illustration of their possible combination.

What impression of truth in poems with supernatural agency?

The relation of poetry to the reader's pleasure.

Poetry as general truth. How is it carried into the heart? Explain and illustrate.

Why is the difficulty in the way of the poet's work less than the historian's or biographer's? [On the part of writer, or reader,—or both? Advantages to be noted on the other side.]

The world conceived as beautiful. Explain how sympathy with pain is related to pleasure.

Distinctions between poets and other men.

Poet's occasional submission to delusion, and the motive.

Objection to saying "a *taste* for poetry."

Relation of man to nature. Resulting connection and contrast between the poet and the man of science.

Wordsworth's definitions of poetry (p. 70).

His conception of the future of poetry.

Why he could not introduce pretty trivialities and ornaments into his poems.

Meaning to be derived from an expression (beyond the present selection) that "poetry takes its origin from emotion recollected in tranquillity."

General suggestions of Wordsworth's character, from the style and the thought of this selection.

Select from such poems as Peter Bell, The Idiot Boy, and Simon Lee, illustrations of points developed in this extract. Also make an application of them to poems like " We are Seven," the series on Lucy, The Solitary Reaper, or The Highland Girl; also to Tintern Abbey.

In reading the three poems first named, and others resembling them, reflect on the reasons for the peculiar impression that they produce. Avoid dwelling only on the side that seems open to a sense of surprise or absurdity. Observe the occasional passages that would give pleasure apart from their context. Try to perceive the real, though sometimes peculiar, beauty of thought or sentiment in the conception, and in each poem as a whole.

SAMUEL TAYLOR COLERIDGE.

[In the passages that treat of Wordsworth's theory of poetic diction, it is well to read such a criticism as Professor Minto's in his article on Wordsworth in the Encyclopædia Britannica, which points out that Coleridge pushes Wordsworth rather farther than he intended to go, in reference to the order of words and the universal application of some of his propositions.]

The logic of poetry. Explain and illustrate.

Test of faulty figures of speech.

Implied principle of style in the notion of an "index expurgatorius."

The two critical aphorisms.

Effect on writing, of an author's "desire of exciting wonderment at his powers."

Illustrate the separate aims of Coleridge and Wordsworth in the Lyrical Ballads; (the familiar human interest within romance, and the romantic interest within familiar human life.)

Illustrations of Coleridge's dilatory habit. How far characteristic?

The class of readers to whom Wordsworth's early poems appealed.

Cause of the "Wordsworthian Controversy."

Remark on Wordsworth's "intellectual energy."

Distinguish between *distinction* and *division.*

Relation of truth to poetry.

Contrast between novels and poems.

Meaning of "other parts of a work being made consonant with metre"? [E.g., closer brevity, other things being equal: higher order of interest, etc.]

Enlarge on the metaphorical analysis of "poetic genius" (p. 85).

[p. 85. "Myriad-minded." In a note, Coleridge explains that he coins the word from ανηρ μυριονοῦς, an expression used by a Greek monk.]

Meaning of "the sense of musical delight." Its origin and promise. Poetic faculties that may be acquired. What beside melody cannot be learned? Illustrate.

Enlarge on the "second promise of genius."

Proof of genius in imagery.

Contrast the two descriptions of the "row of pines."

Meaning of Dignity and of Passion in poetry.

Point out poetic effects in the quotations under (3).

What expression under (4) resembles one in the selection from Wordsworth?

Shakespeare's intellectual qualities; his language.

Coleridge's estimate of Shakespeare's self-schooling. What other view is often advanced?

Coleridge's conception of intellectual sentence-structure.

What difference should exist between the style of prose and of conversation?

Select examples of a distinct poetic vocabulary; its origin.

[It is well to read The Last of the Flock and The Thorn, from which the quotations come. Develop a comparison of the two passages.]

Milton : cp. Paradise Lost, v. 152.

Distinguish between "essence" and "existence." Philosophical meaning of "idea." Force in which Wordsworth uses "essentially."

Coleridge's argument "from the origin of metre;" (styles both impassioned and restrained.) Effect on figurative language.

The effects of metre, and reasons therefor.

Effects of double rhyming. (Select illustrations; e.g., from Don Juan.) Reasons.

Consequences from the view that "metre is simply a stimulant of the attention."

Wordsworth's consistency with his own theory.

Vocabulary a means of union between poetry and metre.

Inference from the impulse toward harmonious unity. Difference between imitation and copying. Illustrate.

Remarks on Gray's sonnet.

Argument from the practice of poets. What further defence may be advanced for the use of classical mythology? Compare Shakespeare's employment of it.

CHARLES LAMB.

In these extracts what traits of the author's diction may be observed? What personal qualities?

Where is his style most energetic? most sympathetic? Touches of his humor.

What sentences take most hold on the memory?—on account of thought or expression?

What may be said on the other side, regarding Lear on the stage?

Cite illustrations from Twelfth Night of the points made by Lamb, and locate those which he presents.

What supplementary view may be taken of Malvolio?

Why, apart from details, are these worthy to be called great critical passages?

[Observe the quotation " Stand still, ye watches of the element," from Dr. Faustus' final speech in Marlowe's play. A sense of its passionate context renders the quotation more effective, adding to what is "a kind of tragic interest," yet not meant as unmixedly so.]

THOMAS DE QUINCEY.

Meaning of "style ; " of " fine arts."
Style's absolute value for itself.
In reference to the subject, its two functions.
De Quincey's brief figurative summary of the abstract thought.
When is style finest? Discuss and illustrate.
Style, the incarnation of thought : give examples. .

THOMAS CARLYLE.

The poet's and the prophet's conception of the world, their subject.
Carlyle's idea of poetry. Is it too deep and serious?
" Æsthetic" had been recently introduced into English when this passage was written [1840]. What would be the correct use of the word by etymology ?
Special functions of poet and prophet—how far separated ?
Explain and comment on Goethe's remark about beauty.
(p. 125.) It is not to be supposed that Shakespeare went back beyond the modern " History " or the old play for the plot of Hamlet.
Enlarge on the meaning of " touches of the universal ; " on poetry's " infinitude."
In what sense is every man a poet ?
Carlyle's meaning for "musical." His conception of an intellectual basis of poetry.
Place of rhythm in language and life.
Meaning of "sceptical dilettanteism "; its effects.
(p. 130.) The Death mask is the basis for the portrait of

Dante in the writer's mind. Giotto's fresco was not recovered from beneath the whitewash with which it had been concealed, until the year after these lectures were delivered.

Enlarge on the thought that Dante is "the voice of ten silent centuries."

Characteristics, under the head of Intensity. (Select other illustrations, from any translation of the Divine Comedy.)

The results of Sincerity in a poet's contemplation of his subject. (Notice carefully how far below the surface Carlyle's meaning for Sincerity lies : a training to genuineness and depth in every thought and feeling, which will recognize absence of the like.)

Relation of Sympathy to Insight.

Illustrate Carlyle's own sympathy, intensity, and sincerity, from these pages.

The style of the passage : compare with one of his earliest essays, and with his more eccentric contemporary or later expression.

The sentences or expressions that represent his poetic gift.

(p. 134.) Guido da Polenta was the name of both Francesca's father and her nephew. It was the latter who was Dante's friend.

The best expression of the thought at the top of p. 134 is in these great lines from Marlowe (Tamburlaine, Part I. v. 1) :

> If all the pens that ever poets held
> Had fed the feeling of their masters' thoughts,
> And every sweetness that inspired their hearts,
> Their minds, and muses on admirèd themes;
> If all the heavenly quintessence they still
> From their immortal flowers of poesy,
> Wherein, as in a mirror, we perceive
> The highest reaches of a human wit;
> If these had made one poem's period,
> And all combined in beauty's worthiness,

Yet should there hover in their restless heads
One thought, one grace, one wonder, at the least,
Which into words no virtue can digest.

MATHEW ARNOLD.

Thoughout, observe the peculiar marks of Arnold's literary manner : his aim and methods.

(p. 138.) Goethe's " Es bildet," etc. (Talent is developed in repose, a character in the current of the world.) Would it be fairer to place by Milton's lines a passage of personal emotion from Goethe, instead of this ethically didactic one ?

Difference between " Style," and excellences attainable in prose : the apparent cause of style in the poet.

Difficult manner in poetry ; " at its best moments " associated with what ? [On difficulties in poetic expression, cp. Ruskin, in Kings' Treasuries, who notes "the hidden way," and " that cruel reticence" of great writers' occasional expression. Point out reasons for the fact.]

Manner of writing in Shakespeare to which exception is taken. What illustrations may be selected ?

In what respects is Gray " by nature" below the high order of his style ?

Reasons for Goethe's chosen school of style.

In the definition of style, expand the idea in the words " recasting," " heightening," " spiritual excitement," " dignity," and " distinction ; " and select illustrations.

(p. 141.) Gemeinheit = commonplace. Hilf lieber Gott = Alas, dear Lord, what sorrows have I felt, from the ordinary man's knowing nothing at all of the Christian teaching !

" A Philistine of genius." Arnold introduced the term to English currency in his essay on Heine : " *Philistinism !*—we have not the expression in English. Perhaps we have not the word because we have so much of the thing. At Soli, I imagine, they did not talk of solecisms. . . . *Philistine* must have originally meant, in the mind of those who invented the nickname, a strong, dogged, unenlightened opponent of the chosen people, of the children of the light. The party of change, the would-be remodellers of the old traditional European order, the invokers of reason against custom, the representatives of the modern spirit in every sphere where it is applicable, regarded themselves, with the robust self-confidence natural to reformers, as a chosen people, as children of the light. They regarded their adversaries as humdrum people, slaves to routine, enemies to light; stupid and oppressive, but at the same time very strong." The term has been introduced from Germany, where it is supposed to have originated in a "town and gown" riot at Jena in 1693. One of the students was killed, and a preacher discussed the occurrence on the following Sabbath, with the exclamation from the book of Judges, " The Philistines be upon thee, Samson !" The application was caught up by the university men. I may call attention to an English use of the word in literary disparagement by Thomas Nashe in 1596 (Works, iii. 132.)

Various ways of describing nature. (Paraphrase the clauses at the top of p. 142.)

(p. 142.) Propertius : The heroes' hand covers the pleasant shores with piles of leaves. Theocritus : For before them lay a great meadow, full of leaves for their rest.

(p. 144.) Virgil : She picks pale violets and the tallest poppies, and arranges together daffodils and the fragrant anise blossoms. . . . I will gather quinces with their soft white down, and chestnuts.

Select from any poets similar illustrations of the different manners of describing nature.

FROM TRANSLATING HOMER.

Meaning of eccentricity and arbitrariness of style. What preventive is suggested ? Essence of a " critical effort."

Poetic treatment of a subject's " level regions."

(p. 148.) Homer : He approached them each with stirring words—Mesthles, and Glaucus, and Medon, and Thersilochus.

Explain the criticism on Wordsworth.

Remark on the comparison between Homer and a Dutch painter.

(p. 149.) *Bonum est*, etc.—it is good for us to be here. Force of the quotation at top of p. 150?

Apply the definition of style (p. 140) to the quotation from Milton (p. 150).

Select from any poems, illustrations of each element in the definition of the "grand style."

Severity of style—its character and apparent cause.

Choice between the simple and the severe in the "grand style."

Arnold's estimate of Tennyson. (Compare Arnold's own poems; e.g., the Switzerland group, Urania, Self-dependence, Saint Brandan, etc., with Tennyson's poems, in reference to qualities of manner.)

Put in the plainest possible expression the quotations on p. 154. Then try to substitute a slight heightening for the bald paraphrase, while retaining its simplicity.

Point out the excellence and charm, on its own side, of this "sophisticated" or "distilled" thought.

Develop the contrast in the quotations on p. 156. From lyric and also narrative poems of Wordsworth and Coleridge, select similar contrasts.

[In recognizing literary distinctions between authors, when each has a high order of excellence, both in his substance and in his manner of expression, it is well to avoid— if we may put it so—liking one of them less, because we find ourselves preferring the other.]·

Enlarge on the estimate of Keats.

Select other illustrations of the "lyrical cry," and remark on the force of the expression.

FROM ESSAYS IN CRITICISM.

Various ways of employing the creative activity. Expand the thought.

Requirements for "great creative epochs in literature."

Remark upon this statement: "Great poets are usually in advance of their age." Apply Arnold's view to Milton, Dryden, and Tennyson.

The relation of the critical movement to the creative.

So far as information permits, develop the comparison between Byron and Goethe.

Deficiencies of the great writers at the beginning of the nineteenth century; reasons, and consequences.

The proper influence of books and reading: at its best is it an immediate or a secondary preparation for creative writing?

Enlarge on the remark that Shakespeare "lived in a current of ideas," illustrating just what some of that Elizabethan activity of thought consisted in.

With this view of "the Greece of Pindar and Sophocles," cp. Macaulay, in his essay on Boswell's Johnson :—An "Athenian citizen might possess very few volumes, and the largest library to which he had access might be much less valuable than Johnson's bookcase in Bolt Court. But the Athenian might pass every morning in conversation with Socrates, and might hear Pericles speak four or five times every month. He saw the plays of Sophocles and Aristophanes; he walked amidst the friezes of Phidias and the paintings of Xeuxis; he knew by heart the choruses of Æschylus; he heard the rhapsodist at the corner of the street reciting the Snield of Achilles or the Death of Argus; he was a legislator, conversant with high questions of alliance, revenue, and war; he was a soldier, trained under a liberal and generous discipline; he was a judge compelled every day to weigh the effect of opposite argumehts. These things were in themselves an education, an education eminently fitted, not, indeed, to form exact profound thinkers, but to give quickness to the perceptions, delicacy to the taste, fluency to the expression, and politeness to the manners."

Contrast between England in 1800–1825, and Goethe's Germany, or the Elizabethan era.

Dangers in provincialism. (Arnold constantly kept calling

attention to the evil of insularity, the notion that what we are familiar with at home is necessarily excellent, and is probably the best of its kind. The man of few books, few acquaintances, little knowledge of the world's variety, is sure to be narrow ; although his narrowness has a bluff genuineness about it that is less displeasing than the shoddy culture which believes something not our own to be preferable only because it is foreign. Addison long ago touched upon this same subject in his pleasantly satirical way, as when he represented his country gentleman's comprehensive faith in Sir Richard Baker's History, and his patriotic conviction that London Bridge was a greater piece of work than any of the seven wonders of the world, that the Thames was the noblest river in Europe, and that one Englishman could beat three Frenchmen. Macaulay, too, just after the passage quoted above, has an excellent remark on the necessity of travel and study " to preserve men from the contraction of mind which those can hardly escape whose whole communion is with one generation and one neighborhood.")

The true office of the critic.

The intellectual and artistic conscience.

In the preface to this collection of essays there is an exquisite apostrophe to Oxford, one of the most poetic passages in Arnold's prose, yet restrained within the limits of prose diction, and characteristic by the touch of irony in its reference to Oxford's inactivity and the allusion to Tübingen, as well as by its seriousness and faith in the supreme worth of disinterested culture : " Beautiful city ! so venerable, so lovely, so unravaged by the fierce intellectual life of our century, so serene !

> There are our young barbarians, all at play.

And yet, steeped in sentiment as she lies, spreading her gardens to the moonlight, and whispering from her towers the last enchantments of the Middle Age, who will deny that Oxford, by her ineffable charm, keeps ever calling us nearer to the true goal of all of us, to the ideal, to perfection,—to beauty, in a word, which is only truth seen from another side, nearer, perhaps, than all the science of Tübingen. Adorable dreamer, whose heart has been so romantic! who hast given thyself so prodigally, given thyself to sides and heroes not mine, only never to the Philistines! home of lost causes, and forsaken beliefs, and unpopular names, and impossible loyalties! what examples could ever so inspire us to keep down the Philistine in ourselves, what teacher could ever so save us from that bondage to which we are all prone, that bondage which Goethe, in his incomparable lines on the death of Schiller, makes it his friend's highest praise (and nobly did Schiller deserve the praise) to have left miles out of sight behind him, —the bondage of *was uns alle bändigt, DAS GEMEINE.* Apparitions of a day, what is our puny warfare against the Philistines, compared with the warfare which this queen of romance has been waging against them for centuries, and will wage after we are gone?"

The limitation on great powers of mind when remote from centres of information.

Meaning of the expression "classical" in criticism.

Discuss fully the merits and faults of the passages quoted (pp. 167-170).

(p. 167.) Bossuet: This man, unaccomplished in the art of fine language, with his rude speech, with his foreign accent, will go to Greece, the land of polish, the mother of philosophers and orators; and in spite of society's resistance, he will establish more churches there than Plato has gained disciples by that eloquence which has been counted divine.

Remark on the expressions "Asiatic prose" and "Attic prose."

The highest test of the true classic.

(p. 170.) Joubert: Acquaintance with a large number of opinions gives the mind a large degree of flexibility, and confirms it in those which it regards as best.

Select or compose illustrations of the traits condemned in
the paragraph beginning "The provincial spirit" (p. 170), or
at least paraphrase the ideas to make sure that none are only
vaguely understood.

Poetry's interpretative power.   What is its other highest
exercise?
Contrast this power of the poet with the scientist's.
(p. 172.) Chateaubriand: The forest's unbounded stretch
of tree-tops.   Senancour: That white bark, smooth and
lined; that rustic bole; those branches bending to the earth;
the leaves' quick quiver, and all that fearless freedom,
nature's simplicity, attitude of the wilds.

JAMES RUSSELL LOWELL.

Contrast between effect of imagination and of sentiment.
Illustrate bare commonplace and "idealized commonplace"
—the latter from the "Elegy."
Characteristics of Gray's poetry suggested.
Lowell's manner of direct and of only implied illustrations;
examples of his freshness of expression, combined with ease.
[Read Arnold's essay on Gray (in Essays in Criticism,
Second Series; or in Ward's English Poets, vol. iii) and Swin-
burne's contrast between Gray and Collins; and compare
with Lowell's entire essay.]
Select examples from the Elegy of Gray's improvement
on earlier poetic expression of familiar thoughts.   [Read
Tennyson's letter in Mr. Dawson's edition of The Princess,
for the danger of pushing the detection of imitation too far.]
Lowell's saturation with poetry is constantly illustrated by
his allusiveness; cp. his playing here with Ariel's song in
The Tempest:

> Nothing of him that doth fade,
> But doth suffer a sea-change
> Into something rich and strange.

(p. 176.) Horace, Odes I, 4, 13.

> Pallida Mors æquo pulsat pede pauperum tabernas
> Regumque turres.

The reference to Malherbe is in his " Consolation à M. du Périer, sur la mort de sa fille." The development of Horace comes at the close of the poem :

> Le pauvre en sa cabane, où le chaume le couvre,
> Est sujet à ses lois;
> Et la garde qui veille aux barrières du Louvre
> N'en défend point nos rois.

(The poor man in his thatched cabin is subject to Death's laws ; and the guard that keeps watch at the gates of the Louvre defends not our kings.)

The second passage occurs in the same poem :

> Mais elle étoit du monde, où les plus belles choses
> Ont le pire destin;
> Et, rose, elle a vécu ce que vivent les roses,
> L'espace d'un matin.

(To the world she belonged, where the fairest objects have the worst destiny ; and, a rose, she has lived the rose's life, a morning long.)

Compare various other poems on the rose as a type of maidenhood's short duration, though more frequently through losing the attractiveness of youth than from " dying untimely "; especially, Waller's " Go, lovely rose"; Herrick's " Gather ye rosebuds while ye may "; Ronsard's " Mignonne allons voir si la rose"; and Baif's "O nature, nous nous pleignons."

(p. 177.) *Tous deux,* etc.: Both disciples of one school, where the frenzy is gentle.

JOHN RUSKIN.

Select parallels to the quotation from Holmes, and explain the kind of pleasure produced, and the reasons for it (pp. 180–4).
Ruskin's classification of poets.   (Has he proved consistent with the principles of his note on p. 181 ?)
Comment on the contrasted quotations of pp. 181–2.
The three classes of perception.
(p. 184.) Cp. Peter Bell, the dull brutal peddler :

> A primrose by a river's brim
> A yellow primrose was to him,
> And it was nothing more.

Reason for the occasional " fallacy " in the greatest poets.
Discussion of the element of " alterability."
When the " fallacy of sight " ceases to please ?
Ruskin's analysis of the quotation on p. 187.
(p. 189.) This passage from the Iliad has been translated by Dr. Hawtrey in hexameters universally admired : Swinburne declares them faultless, English, hexametric, the only true hexameters in the language,—(Swinburne is certainly a judge of rhythm.)   Arnold calls them the best Homeric translation that he knows, though " suffused with a pensive grace which is, perhaps, rather more Virgilian than Homeric :"

Clearly the rest I behold of the dark-eyed sons of Achaia;
Known to me well are the faces of all; their names I remember.
Two, two only remain, whom I see not among the commanders,
Castor fleet in the car, Polydeukes brave with the cestus,—
Own dear brethren of mine,—one parent loved us as infants.
Are they not here in the host, from the shores of loved Lacedæmon,
Or, though they came with the rest in ships that bound through the waters,
Dare they not enter the fight or stand in the council of heroes,
All for fear of the shame and the taunts my crime has awakened ?

So said she;—they long since in Earth's soft arms were reposing,
There, in their own dear land, their Fatherland, Lacedæmon.

Test of a poet's greatness. Is this passage open to question? At the most unfavorable judgment of it, what sound
principle must remain?
Comment on the quotations, pp. 191-2.

RICHARD HOLT HUTTON.

The estimate of style and character in Carlyle, Gibbon,
and Macaulay.
Traits common to Newman and Arnold.
Contrasts between the two.
Summarize the merits of Newman's manner (pp. 198-202).
Moral traits involved in such a diction.

WALTER PATER.

Test of the artist. (Cp. painting and photography.) Illus-
trate "serviceable art" and " fine art," in any literary descrip-
tion.
The audience for whom the literary artist writes.
His verbal obligations.
A summary of the quotation from Flaubert (p. 207).
Remark on the principle presented on p. 208.
(p. 209.) This design of Blake's is in his illustrations of
Blair's " Grave."
" False Ciceronians" : Those formal stylists who aim at the
various forms of rhetorical effect, as such ; just as the main
thought of the Renaissance Latinists was less for what they
said than for a pure Ciceronian phraseology.
The conception of style (p. 210). Its wide range, condi-
tioned only upon what?
Traits of Mr. Pater's own manner.

The enthusiasm for art as a mere perfection of form is
of an entirely lower order than that for truth—when

the two are separated. Yet the thought that, at its highest, art is the most beautiful expression of truth, and
because the most beautiful, therefore the perfect expression,
as has been implied more than once in the preceding pages,
is full of meaning. Certainly so far as literature goes, "style,"
as Mr. Lowell said, "is the great antiseptic:" it is only the
finest manner that compels later generations to read what
otherwise would remain forgotten. When we train our æsthetic taste to a serious, and even an austere, judgment of art,
rejecting every touch that does not en durethe scrutiny of
clear and earnest reason ; and when also we refine our minds
and hearts until they are discontented with thoughts and feelings destitute of dignity, or nobleness, or tenderness, or grace,
or the various other qualities which true art is both willing
and able to interpret, then an application to literature of the
lines of Keats on the identity of truth and beauty will no
longer appear a pretty fancy, without meaning to practical
good sense. Nothing among all the pleasures offered in
the broad range of human resources affords such gracious
and beneficent satisfaction as the enjoyment of the artistic,
or is so full of promise for a permanent source of happiness
and help.

> Les lilas au printemps seront toujours en fleurs,
> Et les arts immortels rajeuniront sans cesse.
>
> (The lilacs in spring will be always in bloom,
> And the arts, the immortals, grow young evermore.)

At the opening of the century Caroline Schlegel wrote in
one of her letters : " O my friend, say to yourself again, and
again, and forever, how short life is, and that nothing has
such a real existence as a work of art. Criticism vanishes,
whole races are blotted out, systems change ; but when one
day the world is burned up like a scrap of paper, then works
of art will be the last of the living sparks that go into God's
house,—only after that can darkness come."